Toxic Asset

Neutrinoman & Lightningirl
A Love Story

Episode #2

Robert J. McCarter

Little Hummingbird Publishing
Flagstaff, AZ

Toxic Asset
Neutrinoman & Lightningirl: A Love Story, Episode #2

Cover image © Fergregory | Dreamstime.com

Version 1.0, September 2014
ISBN: 978-1-941153-99-4

Find out more about this series at: Neutrinoman.com
Visit Robert's website at: RobertJMcCarter.com

Published by:
Little Hummingbird Publishing
P.O. Box 23518
Flagstaff, AZ 86002
www.LittleHummingbird.com

Little Hummingbird Publishing is a division of Arapas, Inc. Find more about Arapas at: www.Arapas.com.

Having the right partner makes all the difference...
To Aleia, my Lightningirl

Prologue

Spring 2025, Three Hundred Miles Above North America

THREE HUNDRED MILES ABOVE THE PLANET, LIGHTNINGIRL and I floated as the Earth lazily rotated below us. Blue oceans, green and brown land, gentle wisps of white clouds.

Beautiful. Tranquil. Serene.

Lightningirl actually likes it up here. It doesn't feel like flying, and the Earth is so far below that any fear of heights is... is... Well, you could certainly be afraid of heights up here, the perspective is dizzying, but it doesn't feel like flying, which is why she enjoys it.

It is also peaceful, intensely so. And I needed peace. While we were up here, I didn't have to deal with my problems down below. I didn't have to delve further into my story which was growing harder to tell, and I didn't have to deal with our current isolation in the high desert of Arizona.

"What's a nice girl like you doing in a place like this?" I signed to her, in an attempt to distract myself from my souring mood. With her coruscating electrical form she looked like a goddess floating there with the inky black of space above her and our planet below.

She smiled and beckoned with her electrical hand for me to come closer. "Come on over here, big boy, and I'll tell you," she signed.

In the early days, a little past the story I am telling you, we both learned a modified version of American Sign Language. It was actually the military's idea. If we were going to be in situations where we couldn't talk, or we needed to do so covertly, then sign language made sense.

We had drifted a few yards apart, so I jetted myself over to her. I overshot it a bit and ended up running into her. She grabbed me and we spun, intertwined, for a bit before I arrested our motion.

Our bodies did their energy exchange. Electricity flowing from her to me in the form of tiny tendrils of blue-white energy, while neutronic energy flowed from me to her in yellow tendrils.

Up here, it's me feeding her energy, not the other way around. We were above the atmosphere, and I could receive solar radiation at full strength. It wasn't the same as sitting inside a nuclear reactor, but it was nice.

As the Earth slowly rotated below and the sun shone above, I kissed her.

Kissing in our q-morph forms is... well, it's different than kissing in the flesh. It is sharp and insistent. It is strong and passionate. It is not entirely comfortable. But then again, with our bodies that close, that entwined, our energies flowing, the entire feeling is sharp and insistent and passionate.

After a time (I'm not sure how long, but not long enough), Lightningirl pushed me away. I could see the concern on her face. "Is the tank full?" she signed. "We should get back down to reality at some point."

I hesitated. My tank was full—we had been up here close to a day, and North America was underneath us again—but I didn't want to go back to reality. I wanted to stay up here with my superhero wife where it's peaceful.

"Tank is full," I signed.

"You ready?"

"No."

She smiled. It was kind and gentle. I could feel the crisis brewing, though. This life of isolation was wearing on me. Writing our story was, admittedly, helping, but I was beginning to think it wasn't going to be enough. "We should go," she signed. "The longer they wait, the more upset they will be."

I nodded. "And they will be waiting."

I took her back in my arms and we slowly made our way down to the Earth.

Chapter 1

The Realized Romantic
Fall 2004, Page Springs Cellars, Arizona

It would be pretty easy to classify me as a hopeless romantic. And back then, back when Licia/Lightningirl and I met, I would have agreed with you. Ashley's abrupt departure years earlier had stalled both my professional life and my romantic life, but I was still the same romantic fool I always was—with the scars to prove it.

But now, from the perspective of where I sit today? Nope, not in the least.

Am I a romantic? Yes, guilty as charged. But I am no longer hopeless. Actually, it's really an annoying term isn't it? Hopeless Romantic. It describes the person who constantly seeks love but never achieves it. I don't know about you, but that sounds like a hopeful romantic. Charging in time and again to let love (or the mere hope of love) kick your teeth in, seems to require hope.

So back then, I was actually a hopeful romantic. Now? Having been in a relationship with the same woman for several decades and still being in love? I am a realized romantic. Not that love doesn't still kick my teeth in (metaphorically speaking, of course). It does. And it does it regularly. Sorry to break the news to all you romantics that are still hopeful—love, she's a tough mistress.

Anyway, back at the winery nestled in the Verde Valley when we had our first kiss, back when our lips first met, back when a mere pressing of her flesh against mine could rock me to my soul, back when that phone call had interrupted the most perfect second date—I was crestfallen. I was having the time of my life and now some damn world-threatening emergency was interfering.

Licia, who no one would ever describe as a romantic (hopeless, hopeful, or otherwise), saw it on my face. I was still sitting at the picnic table after she had gathered our wine glasses and empty wine bottle, folded the red and white checkered tablecloth, and had taken it all ten paces towards the winery. She realized I wasn't walking with her, turned around, and said, "It's okay, Nik. We'll have more time. I promise."

She walked back and set the basket down. A romantic she may not be, but she was always perceptive.

"It was perfect... This was perfect," I said, looking around us at the creek below, the vines above, the beautiful blue sky, and the oddly warm fall day.

Her brown eyes narrowed as she took a slow breath and let it out, pulling her silky black hair back into a ponytail. "Look. Let's not give it up yet. They want us both down at Palo Verde, right?" I nodded. We had been summoned back to my home base—Palo Verde Nuclear Generating Station west of Phoenix. "So we'll ride together. That will give us another two hours." She ended the sentence with a dazzling smile, her hand resting on mine jolting me with a trickle of energy as our bodies did their thing.

My doldrums vanquished, I grabbed the basket and started running towards the large white building that housed the wine cellar below and the tasting room above. "Race you!" I shouted as I ran past her.

WE STOOD IN THE DIRT PARKING LOT OF THE WINERY, THE rolling desert hills of Arizona's wine country rising up around us. We were looking at our cars. Mine was a beat-up 1990 Ford Focus that was a faded blue that might have been pretty before the Arizona sun bleached it out, and at this point might look decent if I washed it more than once every two years. Hers was a 2002 four-wheel-drive Toyota pickup. It was a shiny black, clean as could be, and beautiful.

We both stood there looking from car to truck to car. She was really being kind. It was obvious we should take the truck. But since we were still, officially, on a date, I kind of thought I should drive. She knew this, I knew this, but I just stood there, my mind mush as I tried to figure out a graceful way through this. Sure, the world might be ending any moment and we had been summoned by the powers that be. Sure, I knew that, but there I stood, my head going from left to right trying to find a way to preserve my dignity.

And this may be old fashioned, this desire to drive my date, but hey, what can I say? I'm kind of like that.

"Nik..." she began, "we're kind of in a hurry."

"Right," I said, my head still going from left to right and back. "That sure is a nice truck."

"Thanks."

It made sense. I was paid a janitor's salary, and she was a linewoman for the local electricity provider, APS. I lived at home; she lived alone. It made sense, there was a reason her vehicle was much nicer than mine. Except for the dirty part, of course—I just hate to wash cars (and make beds), the effort doesn't yield results long enough to seem worth it to me.

Licia brought her hand to my shoulder and the tingle there jiggled my brain enough for something to occur to me. "We're in a hurry, right?" I asked.

"Yup."

"Well, then, we better take your truck. I am almost out of gas, and we definitely don't have time to stop."

"We definitely don't," she said, her voice suitably serious.

We both stood there for a few more breaths. I am not sure why. Maybe we were both afraid of what it meant. Man and Woman on a second date kiss for the first time. Man is the romantic one, Woman is the practical one. Emergency strikes and Man and Woman must think and act fast. They both get into Woman's superior vehicle and ride off to save the day.

I was just not sure it was the right precedent to set so early in a relationship. Nevertheless, we got in, her driving, and went down Page Springs Road towards Cornville, heading towards I-17 and Phoenix.

We hadn't gone very far when there was a ringing from her glove compartment. "It's the batphone," Licia said with a smile, "you better get it."

Batphone? What was she talking about? I, of course, understood the reference. On the old Batman TV show, Commissioner Gordon had this special red phone that Batman called him on in emergencies.

I opened the glove compartment and there was a black satellite phone. Circa 2004, they were still pretty big. Licia must have seen the puzzled look on my face because she said, "You don't have one of those? It's military spec, encrypted, secure."

I was still puzzled but answered the phone, "Hello." Seems kind of lame, huh? Here I am answering the equivalent of the batphone and that is all I come up with. Hello— lame.

"Who is this?" the gravelly voice on the phone said. "This phone is government property and should be in the possession of Licia Lopez. Who is this?"

The voice sounded familiar, but I couldn't quite place it. After my lame greeting, I wasn't about to comply. "Who is this?" I said, my lightning wit clearly on the fritz.

"This is Colonel Williams of the United States Army. State your name now or there will be consequences."

"Oh. Hi, Colonel Williams. This is Nik, Nik Nichols."

"Nichols? What are you doing with Ms. Lopez's phone?"

"We were together when the call came in and decided to head down to Palo Verde together."

"Oh... Um..." the older man stuttered. "What... What were you two doing together?"

I didn't particularly like the question. Wasn't the world ending or something? Hadn't we received an urgent call? "Um... drinking wine, Colonel."

"What? Really? You and Ms. Lopez?"

Now I was getting angry. "Yes sir, me and Ms. Lopez were enjoying an alcoholic beverage together. Isn't there an urgent matter to attend to?"

"Yes... Well... We'll talk about this later." His voice resumed its normal authoritative baritone as he continued. "Put this on speaker since you're both there."

I did as ordered.

"Ms. Lopez, Mr. Nichols, we have a bit of an emergency.

The situation has escalated since we called you in, and we need you on site ASAP."

"Yes, sir," Licia said. "Can you fill us in on the nature of the situation?"

"It's Toxicwasteman," Colonel Williams said. I saw Licia tense up and her knuckles go white on the steering wheel. "He's escaped the Florence prison and commandeered a semi full of chemicals and got himself reactivated." Just like electricity enables Licia to turn into Lightningirl and radiation lets me turn into Neutrinoman, Tom Tyree needs toxic substances to turn him into Toxicwasteman.

"I hate that guy," Licia said through gritted teeth. "I just hate that guy."

"We caught up with him," Williams continued, "but he's taken some hostages in a little place called Green Valley, south of Tucson. There's a standoff. He says he will release them if he gets to talk to Neutrinoman."

"What? Me?" I asked, shocked.

"Yes, Nik. You. Something is wrong with him. He's been babbling about aliens and the threat from Arcturus. The media is going to be there soon, and we can't have him scaring people."

I was shocked. The colonel seemed more worried about him talking to the media than if he killed the hostages. And why would Toxicwasteman want to talk to me? And what, or where, the hell is Arcturus?

Back then I was clueless. Now, we all know that Arcturus is a star, the brightest star in the Boötes constellation, and the home system of the Arcturian Alliance.

"Licia," he continued, "you know Toxicwasteman better than anyone, I—"

"Well I should," Licia said, "I am the one who put him in that prison. How the hell did he get out?"

"Don't know, but we are investigating. As I was saying, I want both of you on site ASAP. It's a diner called Big Al's right off of I-19 south of Tucson on the way to Nogales. What is your location now?"

"We are on Cornville Road a few miles west of I-17," Licia said.

"Okay. Nik, what are your energy levels like?"

"Not so great, sir," I said. "I haven't been in the reactor for about a week."

"Here's what we're going to do," Colonel Williams said as he laid out his plan.

Chapter 2

Piggyback Ride
Fall 2004, Central Arizona

L<small>ICIA</small> PULLED THE TRUCK OVER AND PARKED NEXT TO THE road. There was a small bridge that drained water from a side canyon into Beaver Creek just behind us and that would have to do. We dumped the contents of our pockets under the seats. Licia locked the truck and put the keys under a nearby rock. We scrambled down the shoulder and under the bridge.

"Umm..." I began, eying my clothing and hers, knowing they would be burned off when we changed into our superhero forms. I didn't say anything else, just pointed at my clothing and then hers.

"Boys' side," she said pointing to the far side of the culvert.

I went to the designated area, my back to Licia, took my clothes off, and changed into my neutrino form. "Ready?" I asked when I was done, keeping my back turned.

"Yes, let's get moving."

I turned and gasped. Not that I hadn't seen her as Lightningirl before, but something about the intimacy of our outing and my inherent romantic nature amplified it for me. The cement walls were lit up brightly with the blue-white light of her coruscating electrical form. She was gorgeous: petite, well proportioned, and very feminine.

I walked over to her, the yellow light of my neutrino form mixed with the blue-white of her lightning form and danced on the cement walls. We walked to the edge of the tunnel, where she moved to stand on my feet and assume the "slow dance" position we had used when we had flown before.

"Sorry, that's not going to work," I said. With her fear of flying, I hated to break it to her.

"What?"

"I am going to need my hands. We're not going straight up. I will need both my hands and feet to fly us."

"Oh," she said, her electric face scrunched.

I turned my back to her and squatted a bit. "Piggyback. It's the only way."

I was facing out of the tunnel and couldn't see her. After a few moments of silence, I turned around. Her arms were crossed and a frown was on her face.

"You're not messing with me, are you?" she asked.

I held up my hands. "No. God no. If we are going straight up I can manage that with my feet. But we are going to be flying like this," I put my hand out so it was about 15 degrees angled up from horizontal. "I am going to need my hands to keep us steady."

"Oh... Well... Wait. Why can't you shoot those yellow jets out of other parts of your body?"

I started to laugh, imagining what other parts of my body to shoot jets out of, but cut it short when I saw her face. She was perfectly serious. "I guess I could, but I've never tried before, and I don't think this is the time."

She nodded, fear returning to her face quickly replaced by stony resolve.

"Okay then," she said, waving for me to "assume the position."

I went back to the edge of the tunnel and squatted. She hopped on my back, her arms wrapping tightly around my chest and her thighs clamping my waist. I put my arms down straight and pressed them against her legs holding them firmly against me.

As I was about to take off, it occurred to me why she thought I might be messing with her. We were in our quantum forms, which meant we were, to all intents and purposes, naked, which made this arrangement pretty intimate.

I took us up into the air quickly, angling us out of the tunnel and up at an angle slightly to the south. The idea was to limit our exposure to witnesses. Once we were up about five thousand feet, I took us past the Verde Valley and south to the large mesa that sits between the Verde Valley and the Phoenix Area.

There is a set of high-tension power lines that runs from the northern edge of Arizona, at Glen Canyon Dam, all the way south to Phoenix; that was our destination.

This area is high desert, with beautiful rolling hills and canyons. It is a magical area that I always love driving through.

Once I thought we were in the right place, I brought us down quickly, adjusting our trajectory as the power lines came into view. We didn't know it then, but we were very close to where Casita de Soledad would someday be.

When we were about a thousand feet up, I felt my energy failing—the neutrino jets that were keeping us aloft started to sputter out.

"Woops," I said as we suddenly started to drop.

"Got it," Licia said as she removed her left hand from my chest extending it towards the power lines that were rapidly approaching. Electricity arced from them to her left hand and from her right hand into my chest.

Properly powered, I landed us gracefully next to the power lines. She got off my back, I turned to face her, and she directed the electricity into my chest. We did this for about ten minutes until I was feeling powerful enough to get us down past Tucson.

It wasn't comfortable, the lightning bolt she was directing into me, but I enjoyed the moment because we were still alone.

"YOU OKAY?" I ASKED AS WE SOARED HIGH ABOVE PHOENIX. Her grip around my chest was a bit tight. Well no, to be honest, it was very tight.

"Uh huh," she mumbled. It was what I have come to fondly call her yes-no. She said "yes," but she meant "no." It wasn't the words, but the delivery. It's often more subtle than that, but even a dolt like me could tell she wasn't having a good time.

"Not too much longer," I lied. Well, I guess the magnitude of the lie depends on how much is "not too much." Clearly we were already past her limit, so any longer would be too much longer for her.

And I think maybe it was the mode of flying. When we had dealt with the meteor (excuse me, asteroid), we had flown straight up. For this we were flying almost horizontally. She was basically lying on me as I flew us. She had nowhere to look but down.

It took us about forty minutes to do the 250 miles. So we were going fast, but forty minutes is a long time when you hate flying. Even more so when you hate flying and you're holding on to a controlled nuclear reaction with nothing to protect you but said nuclear reaction.

So yeah, she was holding on to me pretty tight. I can't say that I minded in the least.

I could have gotten us there faster, but I thought nearly 400 mph was fast enough. This type of flight was new for both of us. I also kept I-17, then I-10 and I-19 in sight. Even though I had spent quite a bit of time studying maps after I learned how to fly, I wasn't ready to attempt a straight, as the superhero flies, route. I don't have any technological navigational aids, and I didn't want to get lost.

"So, umm..." I began, speaking loudly so she could hear me clearly. "So, did you go to high school in Flagstaff?" I was trying to distract her.

"Yeah," she answered without elaboration.

"Born there?"

"No. New Mexico. My dad moved us out when I was young."

That was better. At least I got a sentence that time. "How come?"

"Construction. Flag was growing a lot back in the 80s, lot of opportunity for him."

And so it went, soaring ten thousand feet above the Desert Southwest, the dry and rugged landscape passing below us. I did my best to distract her. When her answers got short I would change topics. For example, I learned that she doesn't like ice cream (who knew that was possible?); is an avid rock climber (Flagstaff's a pretty good place for that); loves to get pedicures (she is a girl, I know, but an APS linewoman and rock climber—I wasn't expecting that); and can't stand romantic comedies (that was, given my romantic nature, a disappointment).

As we skirted to the east of Phoenix, Colonel Williams had cleared a flight path for us, I asked, "So why are you a vegetarian?" I had noticed this the night we had met at dinner at my folks' house. That one act of perception had been important in our relationship getting this far.

"Is that a problem?" she countered.

"No, not at all. Just curious."

She was silent for a while and I was about to change subjects when she said, "A failure to have compassion for one species of animal, but not for others."

"What?"

"I love dogs. When we got to Flag, the family got a dog. He was a coyote-mix rescue from the reservation. I loved that dog: he played and howled and loved to tromp through the forest with me. His name was Jake—he adored me and I adored him. He saw me all the way through high school before his poor old body gave out."

She was silent then, and I let it be for a bit. I knew I had just learned something important about her. This vegetarian backstory was clearly a big deal.

"So…" I said, trying to wrap my head around it. "Because you love Jake, you can't eat cows?" I frankly didn't understand, but that is as well as I could state it.

"Exactly," she said. I could hear the smile in her voice. I dropped the subject, which was wise, considering that just because I said it didn't mean I understood it. In love, it is often best to quit while you are ahead.

When we got past Tucson and were headed south above

I-19, two Apache Attack helicopters showed up and escorted us in.

Chapter 3

A Sip of Fame
Fall 2004, Green Valley, Arizona

WHEN WE WERE GETTING CLOSE TO OUR DESTINATION, IT became obvious. The TV vans with their big satellite dishes on their roofs, the cop cars with their lights flashing, the dark green tents, and assembled military vehicles made it obvious.

The place the helicopters guided us to was about fifty yards away from "Big Al's Truck Stop and Gas Station." I liked it instantly upon seeing it. It was a relic from another era. One of those greasy spoon diners with a long bar you can eat at and a bunch of gas pumps out front.

It was like going back in time. Somehow this little place had survived and kept its character despite the homogenization of the commercial world.

"A little power," I said as I positioned us vertically, arresting our forward motion, and started a gentle descent. I saw a power line close by and was running low on juice.

This was an important day for Lightningirl and me. This was our first tiny sip of fame, our first encounter with the media. This was the first time that we were being filmed close up.

When I saw the lightning arc from the power line and felt the power flow into me, I breathed a sigh of relief. I really had no grasp of what fame was like, or the crazy pressure it puts on you, I just didn't want to screw up in front of the cameras. And, you know, I had good reason to worry about my landings. There were many craters that marked my poorer attempts.

No sooner had we landed than we were rushed into a big green army tent. We both tightened containment on our respective reactions (nuclear and electrical) so no one would be exposed to too much radiation and no electrical equipment would get fried. It wouldn't work long-term but was good enough for a quick briefing.

"Any trouble getting here?" Colonel Williams asked, his angular face looking longer than usual.

"No, sir," Lightningirl said.

"Good. Good. We don't have much time. We need to get you two in there. Your priority is to keep Toxicwasteman from talking to the media."

"What?" I was angry. Sure Williams was a military guy, answers to orders and all that, but I had come to rely on a shred of humanity always showing through. "Our priority is not the hostages? Not to save lives?"

Colonel Williams looked at me unblinking for a few moments, his hand worrying at his salt-and-pepper brush-cut hair. "Yes, lives are the priority, but you've got to keep in mind the big picture. If he talks too much about aliens, if it gets out, if people panic... Well, there are a lot more lives at stake than the dozen hostages in there."

After the briefing, we made "The Walk." It was a pathway

made by military personnel and highway patrol through a thicket of media about twenty yards long.

As we left the tent, Williams shouted, "And don't talk to the media!" The seemingly endless sea of cameras, microphones, and reporters were enough to make me never want to talk again. It was late afternoon but still the cameras' flashes were going off, accompanying the shouts from the reporters. It was like this assemblage of oddly limbed, one-eyed cyclops following our every move.

I hated it. We both did.

And most of the questions they asked were just stupid: "How do you think Toxicwasteman escaped?" as if we would know; "How does it feel to be a national hero?" as if I could express the potent cocktail of joy and horror that make it up; "Lightningirl, what do you think about the trend of skirts getting shorter?" as if that had any relevance to anyone anywhere; and "Is that his... his... his thing there?" yes, ladies and gentlemen, that is the neutronic version of my genitals—sorry a costume is just not an option when you're a contained nuclear reaction, as much as I would like it to be.

That last comment left me deeply humiliated and deeply self-conscious, and kind of was my first initiation to what fame was going to be like. Because that's what it is like: walking around naked with people talking about you in intimate detail like you are not there.

Lightningirl and I were walking close together. The interaction between our two forms was evident and would be much speculated for months to come. I frankly found her electrical presence comforting as we walked down that very long twenty yards. I was beginning to hope for a meteor to go intercept, at least then I wouldn't have my every move and facial expression analyzed.

Right at the end, just when I thought we would make it, I heard, "Neutrinoman, are you and Lightningirl together?"

I stopped and looked, my head seeking the source of the sound. Lightningirl kept walking as if she hadn't heard (she, to this day, claims she didn't, but I have my doubts).

When my eyes found the reporter, they stayed there. She was beautiful, but in that "too beautiful to be real" way that TV reporters often are. She had shiny black hair that cascaded over her shoulders in gentle waves, red lips, and green eyes. "Green" is not a fair way to describe them. Her eyes were luminous, as if lit by some inner light.

"Are you?" she asked, pointing a microphone towards me, the rapid fire clicking and flashing of the cameras overwhelming. "Are you together?" I would later find out that her name was Diane Madison, a reporter for WNN.

My mouth opened and closed several times in an embarrassing display of... of... Well, I'm not sure what aspect of myself was on display, but it was not pretty, and would be analyzed and talked about ad-nauseam, and make it, in full color, onto the front of several tabloids. It is one of those moments I wish I could change. I wish I could go back in time and just keep walking. It would really have saved me a lot of embarrassment and heartache.

I finally tore my eyes away from her and moved into the empty parking area in front of the diner.

"Are you okay?" Lightningirl asked.

"Uh huh," I said. There I was with my own yes-no.

"What did she ask you?"

"If we were together."

Her eyes widened and she opened her mouth and closed

it several times. I kind of expected the conversation to continue, but it didn't. She snapped her mouth closed and swiveled to the front door of Big Al's. "I think we should face him together."

Interlude 1

Diane Madison

Spring 2025, Casita de Soledad, Central Arizona

"Diane Madison?" Licia asked. "You're going to talk about her?"

I shrugged. "She has a part to play. Just a cameo here, but much more later."

"Why? Why can't you just leave her out?"

I was in the greenhouse with her pulling weeds. It wasn't like I was contributing. Licia could easily suck the life out of them with her finger, but it gave me something to do, it gave us something to do together. Besides, the air actually had humidity in it—something in short supply in the desert—and I liked the earthy, loamy scent of the soil.

It's a simple building, ten feet by fifteen feet, with long deep planters on either side, a flagstone walkway running between them, and glass all around.

"Because I am telling the truth with this story," I said.

She stood up, wiping her hands on a small towel. The greenhouse was her domain. She was the master of the plants. It was full of overgrown tomatoes, peppers, even a dwarf banana tree. We got most of our fresh produce from it. We could get them with our supply deliveries, but these were better, and it gave her something to do.

"The truth, Nik? What about it? What good is it?"

I continued to have trouble articulating it, but in my heart I knew this was the right thing to do. "History matters, the true history. So much of what the public knows about us, about Toxicwasteman and the rest... It's wrong. They are not living in the world they think they are."

"And so what? The world is at peace, the aliens have been gone for years. What does it matter if they know every detail? What does it matter if they know about Diane Madison?"

I bit my lower lip and stood up myself. "It matters to me."

"—that the whole world knows about what that woman almost—" she cut herself off, her cheeks flushing red, and turned away from me.

"I'm sorry," I said. "I know this process will take us back through it all, and for that I apologize. But I have to. Can you see that? I have to."

She turned, her eyes narrow and her jaw set. "I don't know that I understand, but I do see that you are determined. But know this, if your goal is to tell all of it, I will make sure that happens." With that she brushed past me and walked out of the greenhouse, slamming the door behind her.

I was left there among the plants feeling a deep and visceral fear. Her message was clear: if I was going to tell the parts that made her uncomfortable, she was going to make sure I told the parts that made me uncomfortable.

Don't take that the wrong way. She wasn't being mean, she was just demanding parity.

I stood there for some minutes scanning my memories of

the past, and I don't mind telling you I found many, many things I didn't want to share. And several times I decided to abandon the whole project before hardening my resolve.

My wife, she knew exactly what she was doing. She was making sure I really and truly wanted to do this.

I do.

Chapter 4

Introducing Toxicwasteman
Fall 2004, Green Valley, Arizona

Big Al's had a long counter you could eat at with round padded stools that swiveled on shining metal poles. It also had booth-style tables with high backs. I loved the place and wished I was just there for a burger.

Toxicwasteman was sitting on one of the stools slowly spinning himself around. The hostages, there were about a dozen of them, were all crowded behind the counter as far away from him as they could get.

I had seen pictures of him but had never seen him in person. It was clear he was a quantum-metamorph. So like I am a swirling yellow and Lightningirl is a blue-white, Toxicwasteman is a sickly green.

When we entered, he stopped his swiveling and faced us. I could see that the red vinyl of the seat was quickly eroding under his toxic touch. It smoked a bit when he stood up.

"Well, it's about time, isn't it?" he said.

Next to me Lightningirl was tense, and the lights flickered as she drew power from the place. I stepped forward in between the two of them and said, "So, I'm here, what do you want?"

"Oh," he said with a frown. "Not so quick. Let's not get right down to business. How about a little foreplay? After all, I've been stuck in prison for the last six months." He paused, looking me up and down and then doing the same to Lightningirl. His expression and the way his eyes lingered on my neutrino form making me very uncomfortable. "Does she know you're this quick?"

If I had been flesh and blood, I would have blushed, and I could feel Lightningirl bristling behind me. "What do you want?" I asked again, keeping my voice as even as possible.

He sighed and plopped himself back down on the stool. "Really? Are you really this much of a Boy Scout? No greeting to a fellow q-morph, no trading of superhero tips, no bragging about powers? Really? There just aren't many of us and it seems we ought to try to stick together. That's what I'm trying to do here."

"Excuse me?" I asked. I had no idea what he was talking about, what he meant by "trying to do here." Tom Tyree, Toxicwasteman, was a very smart guy, and I knew it. He wasn't some lowly flunky at the Hillington chemical plant when the accident happened—he was the chief scientist. He was one of those guys that were so smart that he could often be dumb (dumb in the ways of the normal mortals around him). So, when he didn't make sense, I assumed it was all about me. What I didn't know then was that he liked to mess with people. He liked to make them feel dumb.

He rolled his eyes, "Oh really? Well I'll spell it out. Look, I could have been in Mexico safely tucked away in a casita by the sea by now. All of this was to get you here, Mr. Neutrinoman."

Lightningirl stepped next to me, tendrils of electricity running down her extremities. I'm not sure where she drew all those watts from, but she was pretty lit up. "No Mexico for you. You're going right back to jail, if I have anything to do with it."

"Sweet, really," he said with a green-toothed smile and a dismissive wave of his hand. "Lovely, the two of you together are lovely. I think you'll live a long and happy life and have many super-babies, despite Mr. Neutrino's distaste for foreplay."

This was starting to annoy me. Why did everyone assume we were together? How could they tell? I sure as hell couldn't.

"But, darling," he continued, speaking to Lightningirl, "I've upped my game since we last met. I won't go down as easy a second time." He stood and cupped his right hand, a glowing ball of green goo forming in it. "One move from you, girly, and the hostages all die a terrible death."

I could see the reaction of the hostages behind him. They were cowering even farther back into the corner.

"You asked for me," I said, stepping in between them again. "So, what did you want to talk about?"

He sighed and plopped down on the disintegrating stool again, the green ball quickly diminishing in size until it was gone. "Oh yes, that. Well, you see—"

"First," I interrupted him, "let some of the hostages go."

He smiled, "You really are a Boy Scout, aren't you?"

"Hostages go before we talk."

He nodded, spinning himself around on the stool to face them. "In honor of our noble Neutrinoman, the women and children can go." He flipped his pulsing green hand from them towards the door as he spun back to face us, one leg crossed over the other.

Lightningirl and I moved aside, leaving the door clear as seven of the hostages left. An eighth, a young man, maybe twenty years old, tried to leave, but Toxicwasteman held out his arm and said, "Not you." The young man slunk back behind the counter. "Are you satisfied?" he asked me.

"Yes."

"Okay then. Here's the bullet, boys and girls. I know about the aliens. There are several species involved, and they call themselves the Arcturian Alliance. I know they knocked that asteroid out of orbit and aimed it at the Earth a few months ago, and I know you stopped it, saving us all." When he said, "saving us all," his hands rose up and flapped in front of him, his voice edged up half an octave.

"How do you know this?" Lightningirl asked.

"Why are you telling me this?" I asked.

"Well," he began, "I know this because they told me. I'm telling you this because their next plan to destroy us is nigh."

"Told you? Plan? Destroy us? Nigh?" I stammered.

"Yes, 'nigh,' as in here, upon us, about to happen."

"I know what 'nigh' means," I growled.

"Very well then, what was your question? I forgot it amidst all the stuttering."

"Why are you telling me?" I repeated.

"Because, this is my planet too, and I love it dearly." He crossed his hands over his heart, tilted his head and gave us a big smile. "Because, my dear Boy Scout, you are the only one that can stop them, again. Sorry darling," he said to Lightningirl, "a little lightning just ain't going to cut it."

"Why, I—" she began, as the lights began to flicker again.

"And," he continued, cutting her off, "because time is running out. Because we are the planet's only hope.

Because I want to be one of the good guys this time. I want to be a hero."

Chapter 5

But It's a Trap
Fall 2004, Green Valley, Arizona

COLONEL WILLIAMS PACED THE TENT. BACK AND FORTH, back and forth. The space wasn't big enough for the energy he was exhibiting. It took just a few seconds, with his quick pace, and then he would have to turn around and go the other direction for a few more seconds.

Lightningirl and I were as far away from everyone else as we could get, with our energy output damped down as much as possible.

"Sir?" Lightningirl asked.

He stopped momentarily, looked at us, and continued his cramped pacing.

"It's got to be a trick of some sort," I offered.

Williams stopped again, his mouth open. It looked like he was going to say something sarcastic, but his mouth closed and he continued pacing.

He finally stopped, turned sharply to face us, and said, "Start over. What does he want?"

"He wants a helicopter and the three of us," Lightningirl said, indicating her, Toxicwasteman, and me. "He will tell us where we are going only once we are in the air. If we are followed he will attack the following aircraft. There can be only a single pilot in the helicopter. He will be monitoring radar to make sure we are not followed."

Williams shook his head and folded his arms over his chest. "And if we don't comply?"

"He will let the aliens destroy the planet," I said. "Just give us the helicopter—trap or not, we have to do this."

Williams nodded, his teeth clenched. He then turned from us and started barking orders.

I pulled Lightningirl aside and whispered, "What do you really think?"

She shrugged. "Does it matter?"

"Yeah, it does. You know this guy."

Her eyes rolled and she said, "Some of this is the truth. He knows that asteroid you stopped had been weaponized. He knows aliens did it, and he seems to know more than Williams has told us."

"But..."

"But..." she continued, "there is more he isn't telling us. More to his plans. More to his motives. Even if the threat is real, he is maneuvering this to his own advantage."

"How?"

She shrugged again. "I put him in jail, maybe he wants revenge."

"So what do we do?" I asked.

"Do? Do?" her voice rose above a whisper, her eyes wide. "Why, we spring the trap, that is what we do."

"THE MILITARY ACCEPTS YOUR TERMS," I SAID.

Toxicwasteman just smiled a green smile and spun on

the mostly disintegrated stool. "Well. I guess we can't fault them for that decision, can we?" He spun some more, his hands waving in the air above him. "What's the plan?" he asked.

"You let the hostages go. While the media is busy with them, we change out of our q-morph forms and exit out the back."

"Yeah! Streaking!" he shouted. "I can't wait."

I just shook my head. "Is this plan acceptable?"

"What? Streaking? Yes, of course. I have no issues with my body. How about you, Mr. Boy Scout?"

I continued to shake my head and signaled to the private waiting outside the restaurant. He opened the door and slid a metal case in.

Lightningirl grabbed it and said, "No streaking today. Now let the hostages go."

Toxicwasteman stopped spinning and faced us. His mouth forming a frown and his face serious. "This is real, you know. This threat. We have to do this my way, we can have no delays. I hope you both get that. The fate of the planet depends on it."

I was speechless. Gone was the loony-tunes version of Toxicwasteman and in its place was someone that was grim and serious.

"We understand," Lightningirl said, her tone matching his. "Now let's get this moving."

The serious mask of his face shattered and he looked like a little kid on Christmas morning. The kid that opened all the presents and was still looking for more. "No streaking, though? Really? I suppose you have some attractive military camo in there for us to don. Too bad." He spun back around to the hostages and proclaimed, "You may go, oh noble hostages. You have served me well."

OUR EXODUS TOOK SLIGHTLY LONGER WHILE LIGHTNINGIRL took the metal case, disappeared for a minute and came back in as Licia dressed in army fatigues that were too big for her.

"Your turn, boys," Licia said, sliding the case to me. Toxicwasteman let go of his q-morph form, right there on the disintegrating stool. He truly wasn't worried about streaking. Me, on the other hand… Well, not that many hours ago I was having a date with Licia, now I was supposed to be naked in front of her. Neutrino naked was one thing, flesh naked entirely another.

I stood there trying to figure out what to do when Licia caught my eye. Her head nodded towards the counter and she turned around. I went behind the counter and let go of my neutrino form.

"Hey. Tom," I whispered. "Throw me some fatigues.

He grinned at me. His human face was long, with high cheek bones and a slim, sharp nose. He looked to be around fifty. His green eyes glinted as he said, "Really? You're gonna have trouble making babies with this kind of behavior."

"End of the world…" I hissed at him. "Time is of the essence…"

He rolled his eyes and threw me the remaining set of fatigues. They were too small for me, the pants only reaching my ankles, but I was grateful for them.

We exited out the back of Big Al's and ran to the waiting helicopter. It was empty except for the pilot. Tom Tyree looked around, a big wolfish grin on his face. "This is going to be fun."

LICIA DIDN'T LOOK GOOD. SHE HAD SAT DOWN ON ONE OF the rear seats of the UH-1 helicopter and was fumbling with the seatbelt.

"Let me help," I said loud enough to be heard above the roar of the helicopter.

She nodded, her brown eyes wide.

I got the seatbelt on her and adjusted it so that it was snug. "Will you be okay?" I shouted. "I think I should keep an eye on..." She nodded vigorously. I took a headset off the wall behind her and handed it to her. "Put this on."

I went forward. Tom was in the copilot's seat looking at the radar. He was talking to the pilot, but they both had headsets on and I couldn't hear them.

I grabbed one and put it on.

"...my instructions are clear," Tom said.

"I don't like this," another voice said. I recognized it as Colonel Williams.

"You don't have to like it," Tom said, "you just have to do it."

"Someone mind filling me in?" I asked.

"Oh, there you are, Ni—" Williams began, cutting himself off midstream through saying my last name. We knew Toxicwasteman's identity (no longer secret), but he didn't know ours (still secret). "Tyree has requested a C-5 be prepped at Luke Air Force base."

"And where are we headed?" I asked.

Tom turned and faced me, his grin again reminding me

of a wolf. "Somewhere fun," he said, wrinkling his nose and showing his teeth.

I nodded and looked around. There didn't seem to be much I could do up here, so I went back and sat next to Licia. I could see into the cockpit, and I could monitor the conversation on the headset, but there wasn't much to see or hear. We were going to Luke.

I took Licia's hand and squeezed it tightly. She gave me a wan smile. For a girl that didn't like to fly, she had already had a lot of it, and more was to come.

Chapter 6

Flying with the Enemy
Fall 2004, Somewhere Over Utah

"So," Tom began, sitting next to us in the C-5 transport airplane, "I bet you have some questions." We were at altitude and heading north, but we still didn't know where we were going. We all sat in the passenger compartment. With its high blue seats, three on one side and two on the other, it felt just like a commercial airplane.

"Where are we going?" I asked.

"Bzzzzt," he said, his lip raised and his front teeth showing. "Wrong question, try again."

"Are you a psychopath or a sociopath?" Licia asked, her jaw muscles bunching.

"Ding, ding," Tom said. "Excellent question, and I would love to spend an afternoon on just such a topic. But, you know, aliens... world-ending threat... and an unlikely teaming up of q-morphs."

Licia glared at him and I asked, "How do you know what the aliens, this Arcturian Alliance, are doing? Why did they tell you?"

His face lit up. "First prize goes to the Boy Scout who can't let go of his girlfriend's hand."

Licia had something of a death grip on my hand—she really did hate flying. Tom's comment only served to increase the pressure. I didn't mind.

"Well?" I prompted.

"One of my guards. This tall, Nordic looking guy, was one of the aliens. He—"

"Ah, hell!" Licia exclaimed. "You're delusional too. Great, just great."

Tom continued as if Licia hadn't interrupted him. "He tried to recruit me, he promised to get me out of jail, I got him to tell me some of what they are planning."

"So the aliens look just like us?" I asked.

"Well no, not all of them. There are the little grey bastards with the big heads, they are the brains, they are from Zeta Reticuli. And the big tall Nordic ones, they are from the Pleiades. Those are the names of star systems, by the way. There are others, but those are the two I know about."

I glanced at Licia, she was rolling her eyes.

"Look, Mrs. Girl Scout. Roll your eyes all you like. It won't change the facts. And the facts are they tried to recruit me. I wheedled some of their plan out of them, and they are trying to destroy us. Aliens are trying to destroy us. You know it's true."

Licia nodded, her teeth clenched.

"And why didn't you join up with them?" I asked. "Didn't they offer you enough?"

Tom stared at me for a moment before he grinned again. "Bonus points for the Boy Scout. They didn't offer me enough. If I helped, they would get me off the planet, but they wouldn't bring my posse along."

"Your posse?" I asked.

"Yeah, you know, Dr. Cheese and Chaosboy. My bros, my peeps, my posse. A man, even a sociopath, gotta have friends."

I had encountered Dr. Cheese before, and knew who he was, but had never heard of Chaosboy. "What are you, some league of villains or something? And who's Chaosboy?"

"Oh, I see that your overlords haven't kept you up to speed. Yeah, Chaosboy. He was in Vegas when the cosmic rays hit. The story is too long to tell here, but suffice to say it was some Rube Goldberg-esque series of improbabilities on Fremont Street that nearly killed him and then saved his life.

"At first he didn't know anything had happened, but he soon discovered that he could bend odds in his favor."

"Bend odds?" I asked.

"Yeah. Take a coin flip, it's a 50/50 chance that you'll get one side or another. That one's easy. He can make a coin come up heads all day long. I once saw him do it a hundred times in a row."

This seemed like a distraction, but I encouraged him to continue, figuring that this may be valuable intel the military didn't have. "The odds of one hundred coin tosses all coming up heads is astronomical," I said.

"Indeed," Tom replied. "But, he doesn't have to counter those odds. Just one 50/50 coin toss at a time. Child's play. He's doing a tour of the casinos of the American West right now, raising funds for our little endeavor."

"And he doesn't get caught?" I asked. "Surely the casinos notice he keeps winning."

Tom nodded. "He's careful, and he's lucky. Real lucky.

They've almost caught him dozens of times, but he always seems to slip away in the end."

"Chaosboy," I said slowly, nodding my head.

"Oh," Tom began with a snort, "don't bother trying to remember the details. The military knows. They've been trying to catch him for the last nine months. But the kid just keeps eluding them."

I blinked, trying to get my brain back on track. This was clearly an attempt to distract us.

"I offered to call the kid Lucky, but he would have nothing of it. With his red hair, small stature, and Irish accent, he's a little sensitive about being compared to a kiddy cereal character. He wanted to be called Chaosman, but I told him, 'You're barely out of diapers, kid. I tell you what, you choose. You can be Chaosboy or Ladyluck, either works for—"

"Shut up!" Licia yelled. Her hand was still gripping mine.

"Excuse me?" Tom asked.

"Shut up. Who cares about Chaosboy or your ridiculous racial stereotype based solely on commercials for over-sugared cereals. If you are going to rattle on about something, tell us about this threat, tell us where the hell we are going, tell us something worth hearing."

As she spoke, the lights in the plane flickered. I don't know if she did it on purpose, but it got Tom's attention.

"Right," he said, looking at his watch. "I guess I should bring you up to speed."

WHAT HAPPENED THAT DAY IS A BIT OF A JUMBLE IN MY mind. It was all so quick, and all so—

Well, I don't want to get ahead of myself.

I was starting to detect a pattern here. "Here" being

my life as a superhero. And the pattern is this: world-threatening emergency; little time; insufficient preparation; insufficient training; chaos ensues.

Tom gave us the bullet: We were headed to Yellowstone National Park where the aliens were about to trigger the supervolcano that lies underneath the park.

"Do you know about that thing?" Tom asked.

I shook my head.

"Well, it'll put Krakatoa to shame. There is a massive amount of magma under there, and it's under pressure. A well-placed nuclear blast, and boom! There goes the neighborhood."

"Can you be more specific?" Licia asked.

"Sure," he said with a grin. "Wyoming, Montana, and Idaho will be devastated, virtually wiped out. The blast will trigger earthquakes all along the West Coast. Ash will rain down all over North America, and the ash cloud will make its way to Europe and beyond." He paused, his grin widening. "But, on the bright side, this will help with that pesky global warning, and probably send us careening in the other direction.

"So, not exactly 'world ending in an instant,' but you can rest assured that the world will be so busy dealing with the aftermath of the supervolcano that they won't see the next strike coming."

"Next strike?" I asked. "What is the next strike?"

Tom shrugged. "Hell if I know. What I do know is that they won't rest until we are either all dead or sent back to the Stone Age."

Interlude 2

Agent Peters

Spring 2025, Casita de Soledad, Central Arizona

AGENT PETERS GREETED US WHEN WE CAME DOWN FROM our little vacation in orbit. He was a balding Homeland Security agent with a sour face.

I sighed as we landed on our flagstone "launch pad" near Casita de Soledad. I really didn't like Agent Peters and he really didn't like me.

He was standing there dressed in a suit, his arms crossed, his mouth twisted into a dour frown. He looked out of place on the rutted dirt road in the middle of the high desert. New spring grass, scrub brush, a few prickly pear cactus, and him in his suit. About ten yards behind him were three other agents, and farther behind was a black SUV they had arrived in.

Agents were never cheerful after driving out. It was a long and bumpy ride. The pathway that led to our house barely qualified as a road.

"Good afternoon, Agent Peters," Lightningirl said after she had let go of me. "It's lovely to see you again."

I saw his frown twitch briefly into a smile. Even Peters had trouble resisting her charms.

"Good afternoon, Ms. Lopez, Mr. Nichols," he said. "Is there something Homeland Security should know about?"

"Know about?" I asked, attempting to look as innocent as possible.

"Yes, 'know about.' There must have been some kind of emergency to justify the unauthorized use of powers. The Quantum Metamorph Accord of 2020 clearly states that—"

"I am familiar with the document," I said, cutting him off.

"Then you must be prepared with an explanation."

I stood there smiling. Lightningirl had gone into our little metal changing shed and come out as Licia dressed in a robe. "Why don't you go change, Honey? I'll fill in Agent Peters."

I smiled. She was dressed in a robe (we always kept robes in there) instead of the shorts and shirt she had been wearing before we went up. There is just something about a beautiful woman dressed in nothing but a robe. I knew it, she knew it, but I am not sure if Peters knew it.

I hate the guy, I really do. It's not his fault. He is really just a symbol, a representative of what I really hate. And that was how this world, this world that we saved, this world that we bled and died for... How this world treats us now. He's a bureaucrat, making sure the t's are crossed and the i's are dotted. If it wasn't Peters, it would be someone else.

I took my time changing. Licia had walked away, so I couldn't hear what she said, but I really didn't need to. She was chatting him up about his wife and his baby daughter. Asking him how he was feeling, whether they were keeping his lupus under control. In short, she was being his friend. It came natural to her. Me, I couldn't be bothered.

I let my neutrino form go and put on the shorts that I had left there. Licia and the gang of agents were down the path a ways, headed for the house. There would be paperwork, of course. There was no way of getting out of that. But what were they going to do? Really? What could they do?

We are officially retired, but that doesn't mean if a big enough emergency came along they won't want us to do our thing. Another asteroid, a rogue nation acquiring nuclear capability, a... Well you get the idea. We're kept around "just in case." We are their pet superheroes.

Sure the paperwork would be a pain. Having to deal with the agents isn't any fun. But seriously, what could they do?

Chapter 7

You Call That a Plan?

Fall 2004, Above Yellowstone National Park, Wyoming

I helped Licia forward into the cockpit. It was filled with handles, levers, and glowing dials. I thought about my dad. He would have loved to see the inside of one of these.

Outside it was dark and we were slowly circling above Yellowstone National Park. She didn't look good, she was a bit green, a bit Toxicwasteman green. I know it was because of nausea, not because he had infected her or anything, but it kind of made me nervous.

Actually, her weakness made me feel weak. Licia is strong and tough, as strong and tough as they come. But flying is kind of her kryptonite—I didn't like seeing her that way.

Don't get me wrong, she was doing her best, enduring the thing that she hated so much. It was just that I wasn't used to seeing her weak. You know how it is early in a relationship. You see the person as perfect, without flaws. That phase never lasts long, and sometimes relationships don't survive the transition. But right then and there, I was seeing a brand new side of her. On one hand I wanted to protect and care for her (and I was doing my best at that), and on the other hand I found the revelation of her humanity a bit disorienting.

"We need those raven eyes of yours," Tom said as we entered the cockpit. "They had to excavate to do this. There are signs of it somewhere down there."

Tom got up and indicated for Licia to take the copilot's seat. The pilot caught my eye, his face grim, his jaw set. His eyes flickered to a switch on the controls in front of him. It looked like we were transmitting audio.

"Anything wrong?" Tom asked, his eyes searching mine. He must have seen something in my face.

"So why won't you let the military help?" I asked, trying to distract him. "Yellowstone is big, they could help search."

"You know them," Tom began. "They would swoop in and overwhelm the place, giving us away. That we are in a C-5 circling above is bad enough. Besides, they are outmatched."

"Can you boys please shut up and help me look," Licia said.

The landscape below was bathed in dim silvery light from the crescent moon. I could see trees, grasslands, and the reflection of dark water down there, but not much else. Tom had the pilot circling an area called the "central plateau" away from the roads and the lodges.

After a few minutes of silence, I asked, "So what is the plan once we find the excavation site?"

"We go in," he began, his eyes glinting in a way that made me scared. "We kick their asses. We save the day."

Great.

TOM IS CRAZY. INSANE, GENIUS CRAZY. AS LICIA AND HE scanned the land below, I watched him. I watched his eyes sweep back and forth. I watched his determined grin. I watched how his hand clenched the pilot's seat as he leaned forward to get a better view.

I know, I was supposed to be looking too, but I couldn't. Something wasn't right. This whole thing wasn't right. It's not that I didn't believe him. After I saw that weaponized meteor, I had no trouble believing that the aliens were about to trigger a supervolcano. No, that wasn't it. I just knew that there was more going on in that head of his. He made this sound simple, he made our parts in it clear and direct. But I knew this wasn't simple. I knew his motivations were anything but clear.

So I watched him. I positioned myself so that if he glanced back at me, a small shift of my focus and I was looking straight out the cockpit windows.

"Something on your mind, Boy Scout?" he asked after about twenty minutes of this. He didn't turn, his eyes still scanning the ground, his hand still gripping the back of the pilot's seat.

"You're not telling us everything," I said. I was a bit surprised that I had actually spoken it. But I guess I had been thinking it so long that it just leapt out.

"Of course not," he replied, turning, meeting my eyes for a moment and swiveling his head back to search the terrain below. In that moment his green eyes met mine, I felt fear deep in my core. It ran through me and I felt a cold sweat slither onto my body. I felt infected, like he had just given me the plague. I felt dread deep and black settle into my heart. For a moment, I was sure that I would not get out of this alive.

"Got it!" Licia said, pointing out the starboard window. "There are signs of significant excavation down there. Where can we—"

She cut herself off with a sharp intake of breath. I was looking where she was pointing and hadn't seen anything, but I noticed the same thing she did: a flare of light in the darkness originating on the ground and heading our way.

Simultaneously there was a beeping from the one of the cockpit panels. "We've got incoming," the pilot shouted as he banked the plane to the port. I grabbed the copilot's seat and hung on.

"We can't dodge a missile in this boat," Tom said.

"Gotta try," the pilot replied as he watched the radar and continued to put us through sudden changes in our trajectory.

I glanced at Licia. Her jaw was set, her hands gripping the arms of the chair as she continued to scan the ground.

There was a sharp metal clang that reverberated through the plane, but no explosion.

"Must have been a dud," Tom said.

"Thank God," I began. "I thought we—"

"We've got another one on the way," Licia gasped.

With a deep breath, I started shouting orders. I'm not sure where it came from, this wasn't normal for me. But this was a crisis. I was a superhero. That's what we do, right?

"Tom, take over for the pilot," I shouted. I am embarrassed to say that I didn't know the pilot's name.

"We—" Tom began.

"Shut up and do it," I shouted. "You," I said, grabbing the pilot and shoving him out of the cockpit, "find a parachute and jump. Tom, keep the plane relatively steady so he has time to get out. Once the missile is close, bank us hard to the left."

Tom didn't say anything but nodded, watching the radar.

I leaned over to Licia, her wide eyes meeting mine. "I'm going to get us out of this," I told her. "Start drawing power from the plane, but not too much, and get ready to change."

The lights flickered as Licia did her thing. I scrambled through the cabin looking for food. I was underpowered and would need all the fuel I could get.

Yup, that's right. Disaster was about to strike, the object of my affection was scared to death, and I was on my hands and knees looking for food.

I found a military energy bar (called a "HOOAH! Bar"), ripped off the wrapper, and shoved the whole thing in my mouth. I stood up just in time to see the flash of light as Tom banked us hard to the left. I was thrown to the floor expecting to hear an explosion, but none came. While I was down there, I found another candy bar.

"It's coming back around," Tom said. "We don't have long."

"Did the pilot get out?" I asked around my chewing.

He shrugged. "There is a light here that says one of the hatches was opened."

"Good enough," I said after I had swallowed one candy bar and was unwrapping the second. I touched Licia on the shoulder, "Draw every watt you can from this plane."

Tom looked up at me and our eyes met again. It wasn't fear that I saw, but it was something related. He reminded me of a little boy on a roller coaster. His pupils were dilated, his mouth slightly open, and his eyes wide. He was enjoying this.

Then the lights in the cabin flickered and then went dark

as Licia turned into Lightningirl and drew all the power she could.

I turned into Neutrinoman as Tom turned into Toxic-wasteman. The cabin was then brightly lit by the mixing of our blue-white, yellow, and green colors.

"I hope you can fly," I said to Toxicwasteman. Lightnin-girl was now standing and I grabbed her, pressed my hand to the roof of the cockpit and let loose a neutrino bolt. The roof exploded and I flew Lightningirl and I up and out of the plane.

We were maybe one hundred feet above it and climb-ing when the missile connected with the fuselage and the plane exploded.

Out of the explosion I saw a flash of green appear. It was moving fast, and I couldn't really discern its shape, but it had to be Toxicwasteman. He was falling like a rock.

Chapter 8

Do You Men Ever Grow Up?
Fall 2004, Above Yellowstone National Park, Wyoming

SO THERE I WAS, FLYING ABOVE THE FLAMING WRECKAGE of the C-5 we had just been in with Lightningirl clinging to me and our ally falling to the ground. We were in "slow dance" position, with her arms around my neck and my arms around her waist. I was pretty limited in what I could do.

If I had been alone, I could have gone after Toxicwasteman, but I wasn't. Lightningirl hated flying, and this day, still the day of our second date, had been full of the worst kind of flying.

First riding me across most of Arizona, then a helicopter ride, then a plane ride, only to escape the plane right before a ground to air missile destroyed it.

Not fun for her. But I had to do something.

"Hold on tight," I said. I let the jets coming out of my feet go and we began to free-fall. I also let go of her waist with one arm, pointed my palm up, and sent yellow neutrino jets out of it to make us fall faster.

"Ohh..." I heard her say as her grip around my neck became vicelike.

We gained on the green form, but it was clear we were not going to catch up. Below us, Yellowstone, lit only by the moon, came into greater focus. It was rolling grassland dotted with shrubs. There were a few streams cutting through, dark pools of water, and tall lodgepole pines lining the tops of the hills.

As we approached the ground and it became clear that I couldn't help Toxicwasteman, I put my hand back around Lightningirl's waist and resumed the jets from my feet.

We both watched as the green form struck the ground and—

Bounced.

Like some kind of superball, he struck the ground and bounced straight up. He passed right by us and we could both hear his gleeful cackling. He looked mostly like his usual Toxicwasteman-self, except he was tucked in the fetal position, and his form was duller and somewhat translucent.

"Jesus Christ," Licia said. "Don't men ever grow up?"

I laughed. I was relieved that he was okay. Villain though he may be, we were on the same team right then and I felt responsible for him. And, yeah, turning yourself into a superball sounds like a hell of a lot of fun.

"Woo hoo!" he shouted as he passed us on his way back down.

"I mean, seriously!" Lightningirl shouted. "Do you?"

I landed us gently on the ground and Lightningirl moved back a step. I was still chuckling. "Do you?" she demanded.

"What? Do we what?"

"Grow up. Do you men ever grow up?"

I got where she was coming from. She had had a terrible time with all the flying. And here I was finally having some fun, and Toxicwasteman was making a racket as he bounced across the landscape, and we were there to stop a dire emergency. I got it. Her question made sense.

I looked at her, my face serious. "I hope not."

She looked back at me, her face first a blank mask, then she gave me a deep frown, her fists coming to her hips. She shook her head, turned away from me, and started walking away at a rapid pace.

"Where are you going?" I called.

"Alien hunting," she called back. "The excavation site is this way."

So, if you were making a movie of this little adventure, now would be the time for a slow motion shot of our heroes walking confidently across the otherworldly landscape of Yellowstone.

Lightningirl, slighting to the front and in the center, her jaw set, her shoulders back, exuding confidence.

Toxicwasteman, to the right. His arms swinging, his hands balled into fists, on his face a crooked grin.

And Neutrinoman, me, to the left, pace quick as I try to catch up, on my face a look of... of... well, embarrassment.

And this is where they would have to inject a little Hollywood into the situation. It's not that I didn't tell the truth—in many ways I hoped to never grow up. I hoped to remain childlike (not child-ish) with a sense of wonder at the world. I hoped to be able to smile and laugh even when the fate of the world rests on my shoulders. Frankly, to me, it seemed like a necessary survival skill in the business we were in.

What I wanted to do was to talk to her. To make sure I hadn't made some horrible mistake, but I didn't. It wasn't time for that—yeah, I know, totally obvious.

"What's with the bouncy-boy routine?" Lightningirl asked as Toxicwasteman and I pulled up next to her.

He shrugged and said, "No big thing. I can manipulate the chemical composition of my q-morph form. So I can bounce if I need to. Much better than going splat, I must say."

She nodded once, dismissing the matter. "Any idea what we should expect?"

"None," Toxicwasteman answered. "At this point you two know as much as I do."

"So, they're drilling down intent on placing a nuclear device to trigger the supervolcano?" she asked.

"That's the size of it."

"Any idea how many of them we will have to deal with?" she asked.

"None."

"Okay. Here's the plan. Toxicwasteman and I will deal with whatever defenses we come across. Neutrinoman, you get down that tunnel and deal with the bomb."

"Right," I said. I had no idea what to do with a nuclear bomb, but now wasn't the moment to bring up any doubts.

We walked for some minutes in silence. If this was a movie, something would have happened already. Actually, right after the slow-mo walk sequence all hell would have broken loose with explosions, lasers, and awe-inspiring heroics.

But, this is not a movie.

Lightningirl stopped, holding her hand up. "Do you hear that?"

"What?" I asked.

A quizzical look came over Toxicwasteman's face. "I feel… In my feet, I feel this rumbling."

Lightningirl nodded and I started to hear what she was mentioning. It was a low rumble, quickly gaining in volume. Soon I could feel it in my feet too.

I jetted up about ten feet so I could get a better view. It was still dark, but the moon shed enough light for me to see what was happening. "Stampede!" I yelled.

Chapter 9

Everything in Slow-mo
Fall 2004, Yellowstone National Park, Wyoming

WE WERE THERE TO FIGHT ALIENS, NOT BUFFALO. WHAT I saw was a wall of them heading for us, the sound of their flight getting loud.

I came back down to the ground and said, "Buffalo stampede. They'll be here in about thirty seconds."

Lightningirl and Toxicwasteman both looked at me. Was I in charge now? "Okay, here's the plan," I said before I had one. "Umm… Each of you grab an arm and I'll fly us above them."

"Can you do that?" Lightningirl asked.

I shrugged. "I've only flown with you before." The rumbling grew louder and Lightningirl nodded. I grabbed her arm with my left hand. We did one of those forearm to forearm grips. I did the same with my right hand with Toxicwasteman.

The sound was now deafening and it seemed like we were in the middle of an earthquake. I slowly jetted us up into the air. It wasn't easy. Toxicwasteman weighed more than Lightningirl and I was having trouble keeping steady.

I really needed my hands. I got us into the air at about ten feet and held us there kind of wobbling as the buffalo began to pass below us.

So a few interesting things happened then, besides the wobbling, ungraceful flight.

First, I have described extensively how Lightningirl's body and mine interact with the exchange of our energies. When I grabbed Toxicwasteman's forearm, there was an odd exchange of energy too. It didn't happen until we touched, but it sure happened.

So, I am a contained nuclear reaction, he is a contained chemical reaction. Where our flesh met, I felt pain, sharp and intense. When I could spare some attention, I looked down and saw green veins against my yellow form as his chemical reaction crept into my q-morph form, and I saw yellow veins of my nuclear reaction creeping into his green form. Our eyes met and I knew he wasn't liking the feeling either.

The second thing, which I almost missed because of what was going on with Toxicwasteman, was Lightningirl. As the one hundred or so buffalo passed below us, small tendrils of electricity passed from the animals and flowed into her outstretched left hand.

I did a bit of a double take, because it is often the other way around, but I was sure. She was drawing electrical energy from the buffalo.

And it had its effect. Those that passed near her slowed down and became docile. A few, those that had passed directly below, even stopped and laid down.

The pain in my right arm was becoming intense as the green veins made their way past my elbow. I angled my feet and slowly and unsteadily moved us past the remnants of the stampede and landed us.

Lightningirl continued to draw energy from those buffalo that were close enough and more and more of them lay down.

After I let go of Toxicwasteman, the veins stopped progressing, but the pain did not end. "What the..." I began, staring at my arm.

"It seems we don't mix so well," Toxicwasteman said, looking at his own arm. From his clenched expression, it was clear he was in pain too.

Lightningirl came over and looked at both of our arms. "Oh my," she said. "Look, we don't have time for this. Buffalo don't just start running around in the middle of the night— the aliens started that stampede, they know we are here."

Toxicwasteman and I nodded in agreement.

"Toxicwasteman, you are with me," she continued. "Let's double-time it now. Neutrinoman, you hang back about five yards, let us take the brunt of their defense. You focus on finding that bomb and... and taking care of it."

I nodded.

The three of us ran forth towards battle. Another fine opportunity for a slow motion montage.

Chapter 10

I Am the Bomb

Fall 2004, Yellowstone National Park, Wyoming

It took us a while to get to the aliens, but Lightningirl seemed to have an unerring sense of direction (another raven-like quality she acquired during the accident). In some ways it took us too long, that battle-ready edge was a bit dull by the time we found the first one.

He was ready for us. Tall, blond haired and blue eyed, he looked just like the prison guard that Toxicwasteman had described, the one who had tried to recruit him.

He stood there in the moonlight, leveling some sort of gun at us. The horizon to the east was starting to lighten, and none of us had trouble seeing him.

Now, I'm not that much of a gun guy. I mean, I know how to shoot a gun, but it wasn't any kind of hobby of mine. This thing, though, didn't look like any kind of gun I had ever seen. It was big, like a grenade launcher, with a metallic barrel and large tube snaking to some kind of backpack. Bullets, I could handle—whatever this was, though, I had no idea.

Lightning stabbed out of Lightningirl's right palm as she

continued to run. The blond man, the alien, went down, his body shaking violently as we ran past him.

I guess I should better set the stage in regards to our battle preparedness, or lack thereof. You see, we hadn't had any tactical training yet. The military had spent time getting us used to our powers, and what they could do, but hadn't trained us yet on how to deal with the kind of situation we were in. This explains, to an extent, the quality of the upcoming battle.

The next wave of defense was three of those blond guys hidden behind low rocks shooting at us.

These guns didn't shoot bullets, or grenades, or explosives. They shot purple balls of energy. And, in retrospect, I kind of think that the weapons had been created quickly just for us. The look of the backpack and the tube that connected it to the barrel of the gun looked inconsistent and a bit jerry-rigged. I think the meteor was supposed to do the job—they weren't expecting to come down here and fight us.

So about thirty seconds after the first guy went down, a scintillating ball of energy struck the ground to the left of Lightningirl. The earth exploded and knocked her off her feet, and sent Toxicwasteman reeling to the right. I was struck by the flying earth, but not harmed.

"Go!" Lightningirl shouted. "The excavation is about twenty yards ahead."

She slowly rose to her feet shaking her head as two more balls of energy erupted with a whoosh and headed right towards me.

I wanted to stay, I wanted to make sure she was okay, but that would have been stupid. I jetted up into the air and the energy balls struck the ground where I had just stood, clods of dirt and rock flying.

Toxicwasteman was shooting green balls of... of something. Some sort of chemical. I saw the first one strike the rock in front of our closest assailant. It exploded, throwing the man back. He didn't move.

Lightning was stabbing forth from Lightningirl's hands at the other two positions.

"Go!" Toxicwasteman shouted as he ran forward, more green balls shooting out of his hands.

In the distance I could see about a dozen more armed men heading towards us. They didn't look like aliens. They looked more like refugees from the Swiss ski team. Tall, athletic, blue eyed, and handsome. They wore what looked like brown fatigues, designed to blend in with the environment.

Four balls of energy heading towards my elevated location convinced me to get moving. I surged up and forward, quickly spotting the excavation site.

Large, low mounds of earth stood piled around an eerily round hole about eight feet in diameter. I didn't see any equipment of any sort. What had dug this hole? Where did the aliens stay when they weren't trying to kill us?

The aliens had stopped advancing and were all shooting at me. Dozens of balls of energy leapt from the ground towards me. My flight path became erratic as I dodged them. Just as I was nearing the hole, one grazed my arm.

My entire left arm became numb, and the neutrino jet that was coming out of my hand stopped. I listed to the left, but was able to compensate with my feet and my right hand.

I increased my speed, heading for the hole at a sharp angle, sharper than I would have liked, but I didn't want to get hit again. I was beginning to think these weapons had been designed especially for me.

Just as I was about to enter the hole, another purple

energy ball caught me in the legs. They became numb too, and I lost all control of my flight. My momentum, though, took me right into the hole. I crashed off the side and started my long bouncing fall down. It went on forever; the hole must have been at least 10,000 feet deep.

The fall was jarring and very disorienting. I pulled in my numb limbs, grabbing my legs with my good hand, and focused on maintaining my neutrino form.

I fell for a minute or two before I came to an abrupt stop at the bottom of this thing. I looked up, the mouth of the hole was a tiny pinprick of light. The round hole around me was bathed in yellow from my neutronic reaction.

I tried to push myself up with my good hand, but failed, and flopped to my left.

I felt a stabbing pain in my back. As if I were flesh and had fallen on some something long and sharp. As the pain increased, it started to burn with a fierce intensity and I began to feel myself radiate with power.

This wasn't right. I hadn't been in the reactor for a week. Lightningirl had powered me up some earlier in the day but not this much. The power surged through me and the numbness in my limbs fled and the lingering pain in my right hand from when I had touched Toxicwasteman intensified, and then left. I stood up and watched as the scintillating yellow of my right arm became brighter and the green sizzled away.

I looked down—things were now well lit. On the ground were the remnants of a metal canister that I must have lain on when I felt the pain and the power begin. On the side of it were the remnants of a symbol. A yellow circle with a black dot in the center and three black pie-slice shapes. The symbol for radiation.

As revelation began to dawn, as my power built further, the earth under me shook and the hole above me exploded.

I hunkered down as earth rained down on me and the aliens sealed the hole, burying me.

One thought kept going through my mind over and over:

I am the bomb.

Interlude 3

Super Problems

Spring 2025, Casita de Soledad, Central Arizona

"Take your pill, babe," Licia said. The agents were gone, finally, and I was headed for the kitchen. I was starving.

"Okay," I said cheerfully. I hated the pill, but much less than what usually followed. I was hoping she wouldn't remember to say it.

"And no cheese, not for twenty-four hours at least."

There it was. The cheese moratorium. There is no food, no beverage, and very few other things in this world that I love more than cheese. And, it was exactly the kind of food I wanted after being my q-morph self.

"Seriously," Licia said. She had followed me into the kitchen and was leaning against the wall, her arms crossed, her robe opened a bit more than when the agents had been here. She was now using her feminine wiles on me. I can't say that I minded.

"Come on," I said. "I am starving. I thought those suits would never leave."

"We've got some leftover stir-fry; that will work better."

In a marriage, it is important to pick your battles. Licia's jaw was set. It was clear she was ready to go to war on this one.

"Just one piece," I said, holding my thumb and forefinger close together.

"No! I don't want to have to live with the fallout. Take your pill, wait a day, and then you can have some cheese."

I sighed and shook my head. I started pulling the leftovers out of the fridge and made a show of taking my pill.

"So, are you going to write about this?" she asked. The smile on her face was impish and mischievous.

"About what?" I asked.

She laughed. "You know damn well what I am talking about. If you want to give everyone the real story of being a q-morph, you can't leave this out."

"Oh, yes I can," I said as I loaded two plates with food, and put one in the microwave. "Besides, not all q-morphs have this little... issue. You don't."

"Thank God. If I did, we'd end up blowing the place up after a long change like we just had."

I laughed, I couldn't help it. "It would be nuclear."

"Seriously, are you going to write about it?"

"I don't know. I just don't think the headline will sell papers. 'Extra: Superhero and his super-flatulents.'"

"That's too high-brow, how about: 'Superhero and his super farts.'" Licia tried to keep a straight face, but it wasn't working. Her laughter rang out as I pulled one plate out of the microwave and put another one in. "How about: 'IBS, not just for mortals anymore,'" she added.

"It's not my fault," I said, a bit hurt.

"No one is saying that it is."

And it really isn't my fault. As Neutrinoman, I am a

controlled nuclear reaction. That reaction will consume anything that is not the essential "me." That includes all the healthy colonies of bacteria in my gut. And that reaction is radioactive. So, just like going q-morph can kill off a virus in my system, it also kills off all the good microorganisms too.

"Super-farts? Really?" I said, laughing. "Are you sure you're a girl? I thought girls weren't as enamored with fart jokes as guys."

"I'm special," she said, loosening her robe, letting it open more, forming a V all the way down to her belly button, threatening to open wider. "And I am sure I am a girl, aren't you?"

"Hmm... Maybe I should check," I said. The microwave dinged, our food was ready, but I didn't care.

Chapter 11

Overpowered

Fall 2004, Yellowstone National Park, Wyoming

I<small>T MAKES SENSE</small>. W<small>HAT WOULD BE THE BEST POSSIBLE</small> fuel for a controlled nuclear reaction? Plutonium, or some other type of radioactive isotope. What had the aliens done? Maneuvered me down a deep hole and given me enough power that I would have no choice but to explode, triggering the supervolcano.

I had to admire the plan. After I exploded I would be spent, and would not be able to escape. In one stroke, they would eliminate me and devastate the world.

While I admired the plan, it pissed me off. As the power coursed through me, the stone and dirt around me began to melt, the chamber I was in growing larger as molten rock pooled at my feet. I couldn't contain the power. I couldn't stop the reaction.

Did they think a few thousand feet of earth could keep me down here? Did they think that I was stupid?

With a feral scream, I flew straight up, the rock and dirt melting around me as I flew.

I passed through all 10,000 feet in a matter of seconds,

bursting from the ground, rock, dirt, and molten earth exploding around me.

I had no eyes for the battle on the ground. I wasn't there long enough to notice anything. I flew straight up, allowing as much power as possible to escape from my four limbs. I would not be the bomb. I would not trigger the volcano.

The earth fell away below me at an astonishing pace, much faster than when I had gone after the meteor. In a matter of minutes, the curve of the Earth was clearly visible and I was above the atmosphere. I didn't just break the sound barrier, or surpass some speed record. According to what I was told later, I flew at over 8,000 miles per hour (or Mach 11, besting the speed of NASA's X-43A, the world's fastest plane—And yes, I am geeking out here).

Right then, I wasn't thinking about speed, or about anything really except not exploding, but this incident was a major shift in the scale of what I was capable of as Neutrinoman.

When the realization came, it was sobering, and even more disturbing was the fact that the aliens, our enemies, had figured this out.

But, right then and there, I was... I don't think I can describe the feeling. I was bursting with power, the sensation heady and dangerous. I was in pain—it was like I could feel every cell in my neutrino form tingling and bursting with energy. Everything had a yellow hue, my neutrino form was radiating out from me and coloring everything I looked at. I was running on instinct. I was so close to my elemental form that my thought processes were very simple... "Me not explode. Me protect people. Me save Lightningirl." It was as if that amount of power had devolved me or turned me into something primal.

And I didn't want to explode. I had a feeling that if I did it with that much power, there would be no coming back. Before when I battled the meteor, I had used the analogy of a popping balloon for how I built up energy and let it explode forth. Well, to further that analogy, the balloon is me, and the way I exploded the meteor damaged the balloon, but didn't destroy it. The way I was now, it felt like if I exploded, there would be no balloon left.

And to be clear, all these thoughts came afterwards. Then, three hundred miles above the Earth, I didn't think. I acted instinctively.

With a silent roar (no atmosphere up there), I consciously opened up a pin-prick of a hole in my containment. This wasn't like how I flew with neutrino jets. This was something entirely different, a tiny hole in the containment that went to the core of the nuclear reaction running out of control inside of me.

From that hole, a beam of yellow light, about an inch in diameter, shot forth from my chest out into space. It took everything I had not to let the hole grow, not to let the balloon burst, but I was suffuse with power and used much of it to contain the emission of energy.

The battle then was keeping the hole small, keeping my containment from totally failing. Once the energy started escaping, it felt like it wanted to keep growing, like water eroding away a dirt dam.

I battled and the beam widened. Two inches... three inches... six inches...

Just when I didn't think I could hold containment any longer, the beam started to sputter and I was able to slowly close the hole until the beam was extinguished.

It hadn't taken long, and I had managed to control things

well enough that I was reasonably powered. I turned back to the Earth and thrusted. This battle wasn't over yet.

Chapter 12

A Simple Choice
Fall 2004, High above the Earth

I AM NO WIZ AT GEOGRAPHY, BUT I KNEW ENOUGH TO KNOW that Yellowstone is in the northwest corner of Wyoming, and that Wyoming sits a couple states north and a bit east of Arizona.

The problem is that there were no dotted lines drawn on the ground, no convenient delineation, no arrow pointing north. And then there were the clouds floating over Idaho and Montana making it hard to get my bearings.

I panicked briefly as I fell Earthward. I was flying fast, but not nearly as fast as I had on the way up, so I had time to think.

The convenient hole with the convenient uranium (I presume, or other highly radioactive material) left at the bottom for me to fall on and absorb. It was too perfect of a setup. They had known I was coming. And how could they have known? Toxicwasteman.

And that put Lightningirl in danger. She was stuck in the middle of nowhere, far from high-tension power lines. I flew faster.

The sun was rising over to the east and I eventually got oriented. I spotted the sharp snow covered peaks of the Grand Tetons and to the northeast of that Yellowstone Lake. As I got closer, I noticed flashes of what looked like lightning and flew towards them.

On my way down I also noticed some high-flying fighter jets and an explosion to the west of Yellowstone. I surmised that the military was trying to get to the excavation site but was being held back by the alien forces.

By the time I could make out the details of the excavation site, the lightning had stopped. The site had changed. The small hole was now a huge crater, with earth and debris strewn for hundreds of yards around it. There were small fires burning in the little evergreen shrubs that dotted the plateau.

I spotted Toxicwasteman south of the crater and in front of him the prone form of Licia. She was naked, lying face down, no longer in her q-morph form. I also noticed that many of the trees and plants around her had this odd wizened look, as if the life had been sucked out of them.

Toxicwasteman was purposefully striding towards her. I thrusted hard, not concerned about the quality of my landing, and plowed right into him. Earth exploded around us and we carved a long trench in the ground with our momentum.

His touch, once again, was painful. I felt the green of his toxic form invading my neutrino form.

I stood up and backed off. We were about sixty yards from Licia now. Toxicwasteman was lying face down in the dirt and I couldn't see his face, but I could hear his laughter. When he stood up, his face made me take another step back.

His eyes were wide, too wide, and his upper lip curled back to reveal green teeth. He looked insane.

"What have you done?" I asked. I wanted to go to Licia, to check on her, to be with her, but that would not have done any good.

"What?" he cried, his fists striking his chest. "What have I done?" His laughter rang out a shrill sound. "I have ensured my survival. That's what. I did what I had to do." He blinked rapidly, his head swiveling to the left and the right. That is when I noticed them.

More of the tall, blond-haired, human-looking aliens. Each with one of the silver energy guns and big backpacks. There were about a dozen of them.

"I thought they didn't offer you enough," I said, remembering back to his story. "I thought that this was your planet."

He rolled his eyes and shrugged. "It was a negotiation, my dear Boy Scout. They eventually made room for my friends. This planet is lost." With that, he reached down and grabbed some clods of dirt and threw them in the air.

"You could join us," one of the aliens said as he lowered his weapon. They had been moving in a semicircle around me but stopped when he spoke. I looked at him and realized he wasn't alone. Another alien, a short grey humanoid with a large head and huge eyes, stepped out from behind him. The alien that spoke had a distant look on his face, and I got the impression that the little grey guy was speaking through him.

"What?" I asked.

"You could join us. You could bring your female," the blond one said as the grey one pointed towards Licia.

"What do you want with us? Why are you trying to destroy us?"

"Choose now," he said.

"Choose?" I asked. I needed time to think.

"Join us and you and the female live. Don't join us and you and the female die."

The dozen guns pointed at me began to hum.

"Come on, Boy Scout," Toxicwasteman said as he stepped forward next to the grey. "What choice do you really have? Life or death, it's kind of an easy decision."

I turned and looked back at Licia, but she still hadn't moved. I slowly turned back to Toxicwasteman and the aliens. I took a deep breath and said, "You know what, you are right. This is one of the easiest decisions I have ever made."

I leapt into the air and started shooting neutrino bolts down upon my enemies.

Chapter 13

What Needs To Be Said
Fall 2004, Yellowstone National Park, Wyoming

I WISH I HAD SOMETHING PITHY TO SAY. SOMETHING ABOUT how raining nuclear hell down on my enemies was a righteous joy. How my skill and power easily led me to victory. How I stood triumphant and exalted on the field of battle.

But that's not how it was. It was war. It was hell. I failed. I fell.

This wasn't a comic book, or a movie. I was still rather new to my powers and while I was powerful, I wasn't necessarily that skilled. What ensued was certainly valiant, but not effective.

I surged up into the air, the blond aliens firing their purple energy balls at me. With my sudden rise into the air, I managed to avoid the first round of energy balls. When I was about fifty feet in the air, I began firing neutrino bolts out of my hands.

This is where I wasn't practiced: flying and firing at the same time. My aim wasn't great and my flight path erratic (the latter was helpful, though). The aliens scattered and some of my bolts hit home, accompanied by the screams of the aliens as the radioactive bolts of energy ate into their flesh.

They all scattered, some finding cover, some firing while running, some going prone. The grey bolted. All of them moved except for Toxicwasteman. He stood there, his arms crossed, watching the battle.

The aliens' weapons took several seconds to recharge, and I took that time to fire as many bolts as I could (making up in quantity what I lacked in accuracy). After everyone had scattered, the energy balls started flying at me at regular intervals. I flew and dodged and fired back, but eventually a bolt caught me in the legs.

They went numb, the neutrino jets went out, and I came crashing to the ground. On my way down, I fired as many bolts as I could and heard several more gut-wrenching screams.

Once I was on the ground, it was all over. I was hit time and again by the purple energy bolts. First they made me numb, then I felt them start to bleed my power away. Before long I was left there lying on the ground naked and vulnerable.

Toxicwasteman approached, his walk slow and confident. "Wrong choice, Boy Scout," he said.

A comeback was in order, but I didn't have one. I stood up, finding that since my q-morph form had fled I could move again. I grabbed several rocks as I stood and backed up, putting myself between Licia and Toxicwasteman and the grey and the blond aliens that were approaching.

It was cold and I began shivering as I stood there above the prone and unconscious form of Licia. There was blood on her head and her right arm lay at an odd angle. Seeing her like that made me furious. I gripped my rocks, the only weapons I had left, and faced my enemies.

"Should we terminate them now?" the slack-eyed blond asked Toxicwasteman. It was clear, again, that the grey-skinned alien was using the blond alien as a mouthpiece.

"It wouldn't take much," Toxicwasteman said, a ball of green goo forming in his right hand. He paused then, all of them staring at me. I was shivering and naked, holding a rock in each hand. "On the other hand," he said, looking at the grey, "the volcano will take care of them soon enough." He looked back at me, his green eyes meeting mine. "They look so delightfully pitiful. Let's let them suffer some more." The ball of green goo disappeared and Toxicwasteman relaxed.

"Very well," the blond one said. They all turned their backs on me and walked away. I didn't watch them. I dropped the rocks and fell to my knees, my hand going to Licia's throat, checking for a pulse.

"Licia," I said, "Licia. Please, wake up. We don't have much time, please wake up." I examined her body looking for wounds, making sure she wasn't bleeding. Her skin was cold to the touch, which wasn't surprising. My teeth were chattering.

What did surprise and scare me is that our bodies did not do their usual exchange of energy. For once touching her was completely normal. My heart skipped a beat.

She had a head wound, various bruises and lacerations, and a broken arm. There was no bleeding.

I moved quickly, but as gently as I could. It was beyond strange seeing her like that: naked and wounded and vulnerable. I felt scared and angry and confuscd. I couldn't stand it, my heart was breaking.

This was a powerful, confident woman, that I was fiercely attracted to, and the first time I saw her nude was when she was badly injured and we were both about to die. Not exactly what I was hoping for.

I pulled her limp body to mine and held her. I had to hold her. If we survived long enough, hypothermia would be an issue, but that wasn't what motivated me. If the end was coming, I needed to hold her. "Licia," I whispered, feeling tears flow down my cheeks. "I'm sorry. I couldn't do it. I couldn't stop them. I'm sorry."

I sat there on the hard cold dirt, holding her and rocking, when I felt the ground underneath me jump and rumble. I stopped and held her closer, not daring to breathe, or move, or make a sound.

This was it. They had found another way to activate the volcano. This was the end.

The rumbling grew more intense, and I pulled Licia's head to mine and whispered in her ear, "I love you."

It was way too early in our relationship to say such a thing. But I knew it, I felt it. In my heart I knew that this was the woman I wanted to spend the rest of my life with. I knew that this was my soul mate—or whatever you want to call it. She had eradicated the last vestiges of Ashley out of my soul. She was the one. The only one. I also knew that this was the end, and I wasn't going to meet it without saying what needed to be said.

As I held her close, tears streaming down my cheeks, an ironic thought came to me, a small consolation in the face of our pending death. We were going to spend the rest of our lives together. Both of us freezing, one of us wounded and unconscious, sitting on top of an activating supervolcano, our last breaths would be taken together.

A brief laugh, sharp and manic, escaped my chest. I held her even tighter, rocking back and forth, and whispered "I love you" over and over as I waited for the end to come.

Interlude 4

Seeking Peace
Spring 2025, Casita de Soledad, Central Arizona

The stones crunched under my sandaled feet as I paced the razorback ridge of a hill a mile or so from our home. The sound was comforting, entirely mundane and normal. Rocks rubbing against rocks, friction, some of that energy escaping as sound. The most normal thing in the world.

I looked to the east watching how the land undulated into hills and valleys and then folded itself into canyons, the raw naked rock exposed where water eroded it away. One drop at a time, over millennia.

Writing these memoirs can get a bit narcissistic, a bit myopic. Staring at my past, examining my life, living in the past.

It's why I had to come up to the ridge. To get some perspective. That and the memories I was harvesting were not at all comfortable.

I bet you've got things like this in your past. Moments when you did your best, but still feel regret. Moments when you couldn't be all that you wanted to be. We are all human, we've all got them.

"Penny for your thoughts," Licia said.

I hadn't heard her, so focused I was, so internal, so "gazing at my bellybutton" narcissistic.

"You got a penny on you?" I asked as I turned around. She was wearing beige shorts and a blue tank top.

She turned her pockets inside out and slowly shook her head. I watched her hair flow over her shoulders and move gently back and forth like a curtain of black silk.

How many times had I almost lost her? Through my dense maleness, through the damn war we fought, through chance. How many times? How many more times would it happen in this extra-long life we were living?

"You know I love you, right?" I asked.

She paused, her brows furrowing briefly as she looked deeply into my eyes. She licked her lips and said, "Yeah, I know."

You may think it a silly question, one that doesn't need to be asked after all the years we had spent together. But I'm here to tell you that question should never stop being asked. Love taken for granted is not love any longer.

"Good," I said before turning and resuming my pacing, my feet crunching on the stone, my eyes following the flow of the land, my heart seeking peace.

I didn't notice her go, she gave me my space, and for that I am grateful.

But I didn't find peace up there on that ridge. Change is coming. I don't know what it is yet, but I can feel it.

Chapter 14

Flying Saucer

Fall 2004, Yellowstone National Park, Wyoming

THE RUMBLE BECAME DEAFENING AND THEN STOPPED. Quiet, sudden and pervasive, came over the landscape. The birds that had been singing a greeting to the dawn became mute. The breeze that had been flowing across my skin from time to time stopped. It was dead quiet, and then I heard something. It was a low, high-pitched hum.

I lifted my head up and looked around. This wasn't right. I slowly and ever so gently lowered Licia's body back to the ground and stood up.

I was weak, hungry, and dehydrated, my belly sunk in from the toll being Neutrinoman had taken on me. The hum became louder and I caught movement out of my peripheral vision. I turned and saw it.

Several hundred yards away, in the direction Toxic-wasteman and the aliens had gone, a flying saucer was rising into the sky, haloed by the pink light of dawn.

It was round and silver and the source of the humming noise. My brow furrowed as I thought back to the rumbling. I had surmised that it was the volcano activating, but it hadn't been. It was this ship rising out of ground. It had to have been buried, or we would have noticed it in the moonlight when we flew above the area. Clods of dirt were still falling off of it as it rose.

I watched with a mix of awe, wonder, and fear. I wrapped my arms around my chest in a vain attempt to warm myself. The ship slowly rose and a different sound started to occur. It was more of a whine than a hum. It grew in intensity until I had to cover my ears. The bottom part of the ship began to glow.

It was some kind of weapon. It was how they intended to trigger the supervolcano. The realization came crashing down on me.

Me exploding down their hole had been plan-A, this was plan-B.

I needed to stop them. I had to stop them. But I was weak and stripped of my powers. Those energy bolts had taken everything I had. Licia was still unconscious, and there were no power lines close enough to change me, even if she were conscious.

I closed my eyes trying to will myself into my neutrino form, but it was no use. I couldn't do it.

I watched helplessly as the ship rose several hundred yards into the air and positioned itself directly over the crater where the hole had once been.

The whining became excruciatingly loud. The glowing at the bottom of the ship became a bright yellow. I began to run. I really can't tell you why. It wasn't logic that drove me but instinct. I think I was hoping that the beam would activate me and I could somehow stop them.

I ran as fast as I could, ignoring the pain of the rocks

biting into my feet, ignoring the cold, and ignoring the fact that I was leaving Licia there naked, injured, and helpless.

I ran, but fatigue hit me and my feet could not do the job. I fell and slid face-first along the rocky ground coming to a painful stop. It was too late. I had failed. This really was the end.

Chapter 15

Be a Hero

Fall 2004, Yellowstone National Park, Wyoming

As the whining became louder, the yellow glow became brighter, I slowly and painfully got to my feet. I didn't bother looking at my injuries, it didn't matter. I slowly stumbled forward, but I couldn't imagine that I could traverse the several hundred yards in time.

My breath caught as the saucer began to wobble—that couldn't be right. I saw a flash of green fly away from the round form of the ship as it listed to the right and headed towards the ground.

The whining sound that had been the energy buildup went up several octaves and the ship exploded in a yellow fireball, the remnants of it plowing into the crater.

I threw myself to the ground as flaming debris and exploded earth flew all around me, some small pieces impacting with my naked flesh.

The flash of green I had seen impacted the ground and bounced—Toxicwasteman. I shook my head in confusion. What had happened? Unlike when he jumped out of the plane, he didn't bounce much, but was soon walking resolutely towards the prone form of Licia.

I cried out her name as I got to my feet, ignoring my injuries, and ran towards her.

Toxicwasteman stopped and leaned over her.

"Don't!" I cried as I ran.

He smiled and slowly stood up, watching me. I could hear the fire of the wreckage burning behind me and smell the acrid smoke it was belching out.

As I got close, I stumbled across one of the prone bodies of the blond-haired aliens and fell. I was still about ten yards away from Toxicwasteman and Licia.

The smell of burnt flesh overwhelmed me. My glance strayed to the corpse as I rose. There was a large hole in his chest where my neutrino bolt had landed. I wanted to vomit, but there was nothing in my stomach.

I pushed down the nausea and got back to my feet. "Don't touch her," I said, my voice coming out ragged and frayed.

He looked me up and down like he had done when we had met in the diner. This time my nudity didn't embarrass me. I didn't care.

"You're going to have to do better than that," he said as he squatted down, his green toxic hand reaching for Licia.

"No!" I cried. I surged forward throwing my hand out and a small neutrino bolt leapt forward and sailed through the air towards his head.

He looked up in time and tiled his head to the left, the bolt sailing past. "Now that's better," he said, "that's what I want to see."

"Step away from her."

"Or what?"

I laughed. It was really a pitiful sound, all manic and crazy. "Or I kill you and everyone and everything you love."

"Okay," he said not moving.

"Okay? Okay what?"

"Tell you what," he said, standing and moving a small step away from her, "I'll give you a free shot, do your worst."

He was toying with me, like a cat with a mouse. But it was all I had. I had no idea how I had thrown that neutrino bolt before, I had no idea if I could do it again.

"Come on, do your worst," he taunted. "Take me out. Save your lady. Be a hero."

Here is the time in the story where the hero pulls from a reserve he didn't even know he had and though badly outmatched defeats the enemy.

Sorry, I hate to disappoint you, but that is not what happened.

I thrust my arm forth again, but another bolt was not forthcoming. I leaned down and grabbed a fist-sized rock and threw it at him. It connected squarely with his chest and bounced off and rolled on the ground. The rock was smoking from his toxic touch.

He made a move to step back towards Licia, and with a guttural scream I charged him. He sidedstepped me and I went sprawling on the ground.

When I looked up, he was no longer Toxicwasteman but Tom Tyree. He stood there tall, gaunt, and naked, slowly nodding his head.

"You've got guts," he said. "It just might be enough."

I rose to my feet and launched myself at him again. His hands caught my head and threw me aside.

I was trying to get up again when he pushed me down and squatted in front of me. "Enough, Boy Scout. Enough."

"You let her be," I growled, "or I will—"

"Yes, yes, I know. You will kill me and everything and everyone I love. Got it."

That brought me up short, and I just sat there silently chewing on air.

"I had to be sure," Tom said.

"Sure?" I asked.

"Yes, sure. While I would love to kill that lightning-throwing witch, I think it would destroy you, and I can't have that."

Another explosion occurred behind me, and I turned and saw the conflagration that once had been the alien spaceship.

"I told you I wanted to be a hero," he said.

"You did that?" I asked.

He chuckled. "Yes, my dear Boy Scout, I did. I must say, I enjoyed it." His grin was too wide, revealing too many teeth.

"Why?" I asked.

"I told you. This is my world. My world! I hate those little grey bastards, and I will do whatever it takes to protect this planet from them. Will you?"

The pieces fell into place. Tom had been something of a double agent and had played both sides of this.

"You needed the aliens to think I was defeated so..."

"So I could get on that damn ship and destroy it from the inside."

"But..."

"Look," he said, his hand painfully gripping my shoulder. "I don't have time to spell this all out for you, but I need you to pay attention. Are you listing, Mr. Neutrino?"

I nodded, meeting his eyes. I hated him, but I didn't really have a choice, so I listened.

"You must take credit for this," he nodded, indicating the wreckage.

"Credit?"

"Yes. The aliens are scared of you. If they think you did this, if they believe you can breach their ship's defenses, they will back off and lick their wounds. They will give us some time."

I nodded, it made sense.

"Can you do that, Boy Scout? Can you tell a lie for the greater good?"

"Yes... I can. I can do that."

"Good. Now let's hope you have what it takes to really defeat them."

"What?"

"You know what the difference between you and me is?" he asked.

I shook my head.

"I will do whatever it takes to defeat these bastards. I will kill, I will lie, I will steal. I will do whatever it takes to save the planet, will you?"

"Of course," I said.

He snorted, "Oh really. I saw you turn green when you saw one of your victims. What if that was an innocent bystander, could you do that? Could you kill a single innocent if that is what it took to win this war?"

"I—"

"How about a hundred? A thousand? A million?" His wide eyes glinted, his voice a serious growl. "Can you stomach the collateral damage? Can you sacrifice what needs to be sacrificed?" He looked at Licia and then back at me. He shook his head and stood up. "I hope you can." He backed up a step and turned from Tom Tyree into the green form of Toxicwasteman.

He was crazy, that much was apparent. I heard the dim thump of helicopters in the distance. Having been transformed with the help of that neutrino mutated rat, my hearing, even in my human form, is better than normal. I doubted he could hear them, so I tried to stall him. I didn't think he should be loose on the land. "Why didn't you just tell us what was going on?"

He laughed. "You're not a very good liar. It had to look good. You had to be truly defeated for me to get into that ship."

"What will they try next?" I asked.

He shrugged. "I have no idea, but know that they will try again and again and again until they are all gone."

The sound of the choppers was getting louder. He would be able to hear it soon. "Why are they trying to destroy us?"

He shrugged. "Does it matter? I didn't bother—" He cut himself short as he looked towards the sound of the approaching helicopters.

He leaned down again, his green face coming close to mine, the smell of it acrid and vile. "We will meet again, you and I. And when we do, I want you to remember what I did here today, and maybe more importantly, what I didn't do." He glanced at Licia briefly before his crazy eyes met mine again. "Our methods may be different, but our goal is the same. We are on the same side, you and I."

He rose and walked several steps away. "Toxicwasteman, wait! Let's talk to them together. If you want to help..."

"Isn't that leash your masters at the military have on you already too short? Mark my words, if it isn't too short today, it will be someday. You are welcome to come join me when it is."

"Toxicwasteman, please," I said, slowly getting to my feet. "You can't outrun a helicopter. We can all talk."

"You know, I don't think I like that name," he said, his grin returning to his face. "Too many syllables, doesn't fall trippingly off the tongue. From now on, I am Toxic."

With that, he positioned his palms parallel to the ground, and green smoky flames came shooting out of his palms and his feet as he leapt into the air.

I stood there gape jawed watching him fly to the north while helicopters became visible to the south.

"I didn't know that bastard could fly," Licia said, her voice weak.

I rushed over, got on the ground, and pulled her body to mine. The sun was starting to warm things up, but it was still cold and our teeth where chattering. "You're alive. Thank God you're alive."

She clung to me with a fierceness that was surprising and welcome. I felt tears run down my cheeks as I clung to her. "I was so afraid that...," I said. "I am so glad you are okay."

"I don't know if I would go so far as to say that I'm okay," she said. "But, I will be."

"Licia... I... We..." I stammered.

"Hush, Nik. Hush. Just hold me."

Chapter 16

Aftermath

Fall 2004, In flight above Wyoming

My jaw clenched and unclenched as I watched her. It was obsessive, I know, but I had almost lost her, I couldn't help it.

The thump-thump of the helicopter was like the sound of my beating heart as I stared. They had put her on a stretcher, a neck brace holding her head in place. They had offered me a stretcher, but I refused, taking a blanket and leaning on a medic as I hobbled my way to the helicopter.

I hardly felt the prick as the medic inserted an IV and started hydrating me. They were talking to me, saying things, but the words made no sense. They offered food, but I brushed it away so I could watch her.

She was asleep, her eyes closed, her broken arm braced, an IV dripping fluids into her bloodstream. Her face looked relaxed, almost normal. The beauty of that face made my heart ache.

I realized my jaw was hurting and tried to relax it, but I couldn't.

It was shock, of course. I was in shock. I didn't know

it at the time, I didn't feel like I was in shock. I just felt... Well, what I was feeling was complicated. My physical pain was receding (I think they must have given me some pain killers), but my emotional pain was unchecked.

I was scared about what had almost happened, terrified to my core. And the thought that represented that terror in my head, was "I almost lost her." It wasn't anything about Yellowstone turning into one big supervolcano and decimating much of my country and affecting the entire world. It was about her. It was about the thing most important to me. The thing I could touch. The thing that was real.

I was ashamed too. I hadn't stopped this. Toxicwasteman had, and I had just been a pawn in his plan. He had used me, but worse, much worse, he had used her.

I was angry, furious, seething about what he had done. I felt hate sharp and hot in my gut, and I felt guilty about it at the same time.

And lastly, I felt like throwing up. Not from my injuries, but from the vision of the dead alien that I had killed.

I was vaguely aware that the land below us had changed. There were buildings and an airstrip. I didn't care. I watched her.

The medic that came over and injected something into my IV was like a fly. I waved my hand when she got between me and Licia, but otherwise her presence meant nothing to me.

The world spun briefly as consciousness fled. A distant part of me realized that the medic had drugged me and a small part of me knew that was a good thing. But, I fought it, keeping my eyes open as long as I could, staring at her.

I WOKE UP IN A HOSPITAL BED. THE ROOM WAS SMALL AND clean, with a window letting in sunlight. I had bandages covering my numerous cuts and abrasions. My body hurt all over, but otherwise I didn't feel too bad.

In a chair next to the bed was Jennifer Johnson. She's one of the main scientists that work with me and a good friend. She was asleep, her head tiled awkwardly against the back of the chair, her curly black hair spilling across it.

"Jennifer?" I said, finding my voice.

She roused herself, blinking. "Nik," she said with a sleepy smile and a yawn. "There you are."

"Licia?"

"She's fine. She's in the next room recovering."

I struggled, trying to push myself up in the bed. I found that I had a lot less energy than I thought, and my muscles screamed at every move.

"Slow down, big boy," she said, her smile gentle. "She's fine."

"I need to see her."

She looked at me, her eyes narrow and then nodded. "Lie back down, let me get a nurse."

A few minutes later I had been unhooked from my IV and had painfully moved myself into a wheelchair. Jennifer pushed me into the next room.

Licia Lopez was asleep, her arm in a cast. I stared at her face and felt... God, this is hard. It's hard to explain these emotions. We were so early in our relationship, but out there in the battle, out there when it looked like there would be no tomorrow, it became clear to me that I loved her. And not in some small way. I LOVED her with a passion that I didn't know I was capable of, a passion that eclipsed anything I had ever felt before.

I stared at her face. The long dark lashes, her smooth, light brown skin, her jet-black hair arrayed awkwardly. I drank her in like I was in a desert and looking at her was water. I felt my heart in a way that I had never felt it before: both tender and hard at the same time. I had no idea that love was like this, that you could feel like this.

It was painful and glorious at the same time.

"She's okay," Jennifer whispered. She had squatted down next to me.

"What are her injuries?" I asked.

"A concussion, a broken arm, broken ribs, lots of bruises, cuts and abrasions. She's fine, Nik. I swear to you she is fine"

"I... I love her."

Jennifer smiled and nodded, "I know."

"How?"

She chuckled. "Everyone knows, Nik. It's the most obvious thing in the world."

"Do you think she knows?" I asked. I mean, I was just figuring this out, what if she knew and didn't feel the same way?

Jennifer smiled back in response. Of course Licia knew, she was a woman and women are better at this feeling stuff than men.

We stayed there for a long time until I started dozing off and couldn't resist being taken back to my own room.

IT WAS LIKE A SCENE FROM SOME STEVEN SPIELBERG sci-fi movie: helicopters flying overhead, tents teeming with military personnel, scientists in white coats with odd-looking instruments. They ran around the landscape of Yellowstone like ants searching for food and bringing it back to their nest.

Licia looked tired and drawn, but she was on her feet. I was tired too—no reactor time yet, which is what I needed to feel better. They had flown us out here after several days in the Francis E. Warren Air Force infirmary.

Williams and a few others were debriefing us. They were taking Licia's statement first. I had mostly tuned it out. This place made me feel numb. I had trouble concentrating. My ears perked up when she started talking about what happened when I was in the hole.

"They changed their weapons," she said. "They were shooting those purple balls of energy at Nik. I got grazed a few times by them, and they didn't hurt me at all. After he left, they changed them to shooting these pale orange balls of energy. Those hurt, those sucked what little energy I had. The first one hit my right arm, it went numb."

Williams nodded and asked, "And Toxicwasteman?"

She snorted, but it wasn't derisive or humorous. It was a defeated I-told-you-so kind of a sound. "He started firing his green balls of goo at me, but they all missed. He wasn't fully focused on me, he kept glancing back to the hole. It was clear he was with them."

"Did they speak?"

She nodded. "They seemed to be taking orders from him. He told them when to trigger the explosion, the one that buried Nik in there. One of them stopped firing and pulled out a small device. The ground shook, and the crater formed." She pointed over to the large depression of land.

I looked and blinked. It seemed like it had all just happened and that it was ancient history at the same time. The wreckage of the alien ship was strewn around the landscape to the right of the crater. It was still smoldering and people in hazmat suits swarmed around it, the ants looking for more treasures.

"Was your lightning effective against the aliens?" William asked.

She nodded. "Yeah, it was. It took some doing. I think their clothing protected them some. You know, Colonel, they were expecting us. They were ready for us."

Williams nodded, a grim look on his face. "I know."

I noticed the odd trees around the area. They looked wizened and desiccated. They looked like they had been sucked dry. I recall seeing an alien or two that looked like that.

"Did you do this?" I asked her, pointing at one of the trees. I remembered how she had drawn electricity from the buffalo and that had calmed them.

"I did," she said. "I had no good source of electricity, so I drew it from the surroundings."

Licia continued to describe the battle, but I walked away. I didn't want to hear it. I already knew what happened. They overwhelmed her. They hurt her.

My feet carried me towards the crater until the marker on the ground stopped me. There was a white outline sprayed on the dirt in the shape of a prone body. The maker was yellow and written on it was "Hostile #5."

I remembered him. I had tripped over him on my way to try to stop Toxicwasteman from hurting Licia. He had taken a neutrino bolt to the chest and was dead, the hole ragged and red with bits of bone sticking out. His corpse had smelled like badly burnt barbecue. I stood there, my eyes blinking rapidly, remembering what it felt like when my foot collided with his lifeless body.

The memory of him came back in a flash. He had leveled

his energy weapon at me, a purple ball flying from it towards my chest. I had thrown myself to the right, a neutrino jet coming out of my left hand to keep me from falling to the ground, while a neutrino bolt fired out of my right hand. I remembered seeing the bolt connect with his flesh, hearing him scream, being vaguely fascinated at how round a hole it had made, at how the edges of his clothing smoked, of how he fell to the ground like some sort of puppet with its strings cut.

I felt nausea rise and managed to stumble a few more yards away before I vomited.

His face, his handsome, blond-haired, blue-eyed face, I can still see it in my mind. I can still see the look of surprise when the yellow bolt hit him, when his life fled, when I killed him.

After I had emptied the contents of my stomach, I wept. The tears were hot and bitter and I did nothing to stop them. I couldn't. I had crossed a boundary, one I couldn't come back from. I had looked a being in the eye and killed him. My world had changed, I had changed.

I knew I was making a scene, and some part of me knew it was the trauma, but I didn't care. I couldn't care about it then. I could only sit there on the cold ground weeping.

Jennifer came and put a blanket around me, gave me water and a handkerchief, and sat there with me. She didn't speak, she didn't try to stop me burbling, she just watched over me and kept others away.

I promised you the real story, the whole story, what it was really like to be a superhero in those times. And that is what it was like. Sometimes it was sitting on the ground crying your eyes out because of what you did, because of the trauma you had suffered.

And I know that this was war, that we all view killing differently in a war. I know that he was an alien, that he was trying to destroy our planet. I know all that.

And you know what? Those are fine intellectual concepts, but bullshit when it comes to being human. The emotions can't be denied, or at least not for too long.

I kept seeing his face and those wide blue eyes, how surprised they looked when the neutrino bolt connected with him. I kept seeing and smelling the corpse when I stumbled over it, kept feeling my foot against his inert flesh.

He was my first but not my last.

Chapter 17

Complicated

Fall 2004, Francis E. Warren Air Force Base, Wyoming

THE AIR WAS COOL BUT REFRESHING. THE SUN SHONE brightly, and I soaked it up. Licia and I were walking just outside the infirmary at the Francis E. Warren Air Force Base in Cheyenne, Wyoming.

Jennifer was a discreet distance away with a wheelchair in case one of us needed it. It had taken nearly a presidential decree from the powers that be to let us out of the building for a walk. Well, not a presidential decree, but a look of grim determination in Licia's eyes that even Colonel Williams was not inclined to deny.

Our conversations had been awkward so far. You know, how we were both feeling, the weather, nothing that mattered. I felt this shyness that I couldn't explain. Well, now I can explain it. I knew that I loved her. I knew that I needed to tell her, but I was scared to death of her not returning the sentiment.

"So..." I said after a long pause. We had found a bench to sit on.

"Yeah," she answered.

"Listen… I realized something out there. Something important. Something I need to tell you."

"Me too," she said nodding her head.

"Oh… Okay. Ladies first."

She pursed her lips and looked at me. Her brown eyes were so sad, I felt my stomach clench at the sight. "This thing with the aliens," she began. "This war. It's… It's not what I expected. It's much harder, much more complicated than I thought."

I nodded in agreement. "I couldn't have said it better."

She stared at me, her brow briefly furrowing before looking away. "And there is no doubt that we are going to be working together… Going into battle together…"

I bit my lip and nodded as fear gripped me. Despite the cold, I was sweating.

"We have to have clear heads. We have to make the right choices. We…" She trailed off, her brown eyes meeting mine again. They were moist with tears. I knew what was coming.

"Wait," I said. "Stop. Please, don't say it."

"Nik. We can't keep—"

"No!" I stood up and paced slowly in front of her. "Look, I realized something out there. And before you say what you are going to say, I have to tell you. I have to—" I kneeled in front of her and took her hand, squeezing it. She didn't resist, but she didn't squeeze back either. The typical electrical sensation, though, was coming back as we healed, and that was a relief.

"I never expected this," I began. "Not since the accident. I never expected to find someone that I was compatible with. To find someone that made me more than I am alone." I raised my hand so it was an inch from hers and a thin white tendril of energy jumped from her skin to mine as a tiny yellow tendril jumped from my hand to hers. "Look, Licia, look. We are meant to be together. We go together."

She grabbed my hand, closing the connection and squeezing hard. Her eyes met mine. The sadness was still there, but this time they were fierce. "I can't, Nik. I can't feel like that about you and do what we need to do. I can't, I'm sorry."

"But... Licia, I love you. I have never felt anything like this before. I love you."

"I'm sorry, Nik." Tears were rolling down her face as she stood up and walked away, leaving me there kneeling in front of an empty bench.

IT WAS STUPID TO BE OUT IN THE COLD AND I KNEW IT, but I couldn't go back into the infirmary. I couldn't risk seeing her.

Yeah, I know. This is the point in the movie where you just can't believe how stupid the romantic lead is being. When you feel like shouting at the screen, "Go get her, you fool! What are you waiting for? Despite what she said, she loves you."

And in retrospect, I agree with you. As I am writing this, I too am shouting at my former self. From the perspective of where I sit today, going after her was the right thing to do.

But the me that was there, huddled on the bench shivering, couldn't do anything about it. I was traumatized from the recent battle with Toxicwasteman and the aliens, and my heart was broken.

So I sat there, cold creeping into my aching body, and stared at the ground.

"Let's go," Jennifer said, wrapping a blanket around me.

"I'm not going back in there," I told her.

"I know," she said. Her smile and the compassion on her face made me look away. "We're going back to Palo Verde. You're well enough to handle some radiation. It will help you heal."

I looked up at her and shook my head. The kind of healing I needed wasn't the kind that Palo Verde Nuclear Generating Station could give.

Chapter 18

What We Fight For
Winter 2004, Central Arizona

THE ROLLING HILLS OF CENTRAL ARIZONA LAY BEFORE ME. The winter grasses were brown, and the sky above was a piercing blue. I paced in a tight circle, the ground below my neutrino feet slowly transforming into something lava-like.

I was scared—deep in my belly, fear was running wild. Give me a world-ending meteor or murderous aliens any day. Even give me Toxicwasteman. Better than this. Much better than this.

My nervousness was compounded by the fact that it had taken me months to work up the nerve to do this. Women can make you strong, but they can also make you weak. Ashley's leaving all those years ago had made me weak. I had let her go without a fight. I was not going to do the same thing with Licia. But to say that Ashley wasn't part of my reticence would be a lie. We all drag our past into the present with us.

I heard her approach. The crackling of electricity flowing down the high-tension power lines from the south. There was then the flash of lightning and the crack of thunder and she was standing in front of me.

Lightningirl. The coruscating electrical form of a goddess.

I blinked rapidly. As Neutrinoman, I am not biological, I cannot cry, and for that I was grateful. I could, though, still feel a full array of human emotions.

I smiled as best I could and said, "Thank you for coming."

She looked around. This was the same spot she had charged me at the end of our second date before we flew off to deal with Toxicwasteman. She nodded slowly. "It's nice here. Peaceful."

I almost followed up on that. It would be so much easier to chat about the beauty of the land or the weather. But that is not what I was here for.

"If you don't mind," I began, "I am going to get right to it."

Her expression was bland and inscrutable as she said, "Please."

The silence grew thick as I struggled with how to begin. I knew her well enough to know that I would have only one chance at this. That I had to get it right. Yeah, no pressure there.

"Nik?" she said after a time.

I stopped my pacing and looked at her. I'm the romantic, she is not. Even back then I was getting a view of that. I needed to appeal to her practical side.

I smiled and shook my head and began. "Our lives are not normal. We have these powers. We are living in this time, in the middle of this war fighting an enemy we don't understand."

She nodded her head in agreement.

"The stakes are high. And the one thought that keeps

going through my head is: what am I fighting for? It would be easy to say that I am fighting for the Earth, for the entire human race. And I am, but that is so distant, so ephemeral. That is not where I will go when I need courage. When I need strength.

"I will look to what I am really fighting for. My family. My friends. My loved ones. I will fight for the things that really matter.

"And when I fight, when I am out there making hard choices, doing my best, win or lose, I will be fighting for you, Licia."

"Nik," she began. "Please..."

"I will. You think that love will somehow lead us down the wrong path. Make us weak. Cause us to make the wrong decisions. But I don't see that. Love makes us strong. Love gives us reason to get out there and do what we need to do."

She opened her mouth to speak, but I forged on.

"And it doesn't matter if we are a couple. It doesn't. I will fight for you and my parents and my friends. I will fight for Sunday barbecues and winter skiing trips. I will fight for starry nights with nothing to do but stare up at the sky. I will fight for giggling babies and smiling seniors. I will fight, Licia, for you."

She nodded, her brows furrowed. "But can you do what you have to do for the planet? Could you sacrifice me, if that is what it took?"

"Yes," I answered without hesitation.

She looked at me intently. She didn't believe me. "I was awake, you know," she said. "Out there in Yellowstone with Toxicwasteman. I heard some of that."

"Good," I said. "Then you know that his threatening you gave me strength."

"It also made you stupid," she said.

My jaw dropped and I stared at her.

"You attacked him in your biological form to try to protect me," she continued. "When there was no chance you could defeat him. When he could have easily killed you."

I tried to speak, but couldn't, my mouth moving in a mute pantomime. Thoughts raged in my mind, but nothing more than incoherent fragments.

"I care for you, Nik. I do. I just don't think this is a good idea." With a sharp crack and a flash of lightning, she was gone.

I took a moment, okay a few minutes, to stand there in despair. I then screamed and raged and pounded the ground. I kicked rocks and shot neutrino bolts at innocent shrubs. It wasn't completely effective, but I did my best to get it out of my system.

I then took a deep breath and hardened my resolve. I had two battles to fight. One for the planet and one for Licia's heart.

Epilogue

Spring 2025, Casita de Soledad, Central Arizona

"W<small>ELL</small>?" I <small>ASKED AFTER</small> L<small>ICIA FINISHED READING THE</small> manuscript. The soft whisper of the pages moving as she read had ended several minutes ago, and I was getting anxious.

We were in the greenhouse. Licia had been occupying herself a lot lately with gardening. I spend my days writing, she spends her days growing plants.

It seems a little... what's the right word? It seems a little "pedestrian." I am not saying there is anything wrong with either activity, but after the life we've had, it's just so small.

Not that Licia can't grow plants. At this point she has a subtle control over her use of electricity and can perk up a tomato plant just as easily as she can suck the life out of a weed.

She was sitting on the flagstone floor of the greenhouse looking kind of pale.

"I..." she began.

She flipped back a few pages and read again. From that reaction, I was desperate to ask her what had happened.

What was wrong, but I didn't. Through long experience I had learned to give her space when she needed it.

She dropped the papers, stood up and hugged me. It wasn't a romantic hug, it was a fierce one. As if by holding me tightly enough she could ward off what she was feeling. "I am so sorry," she whispered.

I was still confused, but my lack of understanding didn't seem important. I returned her hug and whispered back, "It's okay."

She held me for several minutes before stepping back. "You don't have any idea what I'm sorry about, do you?"

I shrugged my shoulders. It would do me no good to deny it; she knew me too well. "No, I don't."

She went back to the sheaf of papers and shuffled through them and pointed at a passage. It was where I made my rather laughable attempt to run naked across the Yellowstone landscape to intercept the pending energy beam from the spaceship. "Kinda lame, huh?" I said. "Actually, it's kind of embarrassing to write about—"

She put her finger on my lips, cutting me off. Her face was a play of guilt and surprise. Her eyebrows furrowed and tears began to flow down her cheeks. "You left me..." she began.

I was worried then. Tears are the danger zone. It can be really good or really bad, and I had no clue which one this was. "Yeah. You know the world was going to end... Last desperate gamble..."

She laughed, throwing the papers into the air. They floated down, landing on the tomato and pepper plants, making a rather huge mess.

"I had to try. I had to do something," I said by way of

explanation. "I couldn't just watch the aliens turn Wyoming into a volcano. I—"

"God, I am so sorry. I was so hard on you. I came to right at the end there, right when it looked like you were throwing your life away to save mine. I missed you leaving me there alone and injured and vulnerable."

I started to speak several times, but cut myself off. I was too damn confused to say anything intelligent. "Honey, I need you to pretend that I am stupid when it comes to the ways of a woman's heart. Please explain this to me in short sentences, using small words."

She smiled, tears returning. "I broke up with you because I witnessed you, the flesh and blood you, trying to take on Toxicwasteman. It looked like you were willing to throw your life away to save me."

"Yeah..." I said, more as a prompt for her to continue than in agreement.

"And right before that you had left me. Put my life at risk to try to save us all."

"Right," I said, trying to keep my face as neutral as possible. I was still confused. This didn't seem like a revelation to me; that is what happened.

She laughed and bumped me in the chest. "Jesus, Nik. Don't you get it? If I had witnessed it all, if I had known. I wouldn't... I wouldn't have broken up with you. We could have avoided a whole lot of crap."

"Oh," I said, my face falling as I finally understood. We had never talked about what happened that day. Between the pace of upcoming events and the trauma of that day, we just never got to it.

"I am so sorry," she said. "Can you forgive me?"

I sighed heavily and looked down, furrowing my brow. "I... Well..."

"Please, Nik. I feel like such a fool. I'll do anything... anything."

And in truth the realization did hurt. That we could have avoided a lot of heartache with a little communication was hard to swallow. But it was also twenty years ago and a minor bump in the very long road of our relationship. "Anything?" I asked, my head still down, but I couldn't keep the smile from forming on my lips.

"Oh, hell," she said, catching the smile on my face. "You're gonna milk this for all it's worth."

"That I am," I said, raising my head.

She crossed her arms and said, "Okay, what is it that you want?"

I looked up into the sky, the sun shining on my face. "First, I want to go up more often. A lot more often."

"Then Peters will be here a lot more often."

I shrugged. "We need to start training them. They need to understand we aren't their pet superheroes."

"Okay. What else?"

I shook my head, blinking back tears. I was remembering that day, not far from here, when she had broken my heart. I have perspective on those events now. Toxicwasteman, the aliens, Yellowstone, realizing my love for Licia and her rejecting me. It was the forge, the fire, that made me. It was painful and difficult, but with what came after it, I now see it as necessary.

I'm not one to regret the past. I have had an incredible life, and many parts of it were difficult and traumatic, but they made me who I am.

"Nothing," I said. "You don't have to feel bad or be sorry. We were all going through so much."

She nodded and took my hand. "Let's go for walk."

We took the trail to our launching pad, to the power lines, and she began following them to the north. I knew where she was taking me.

I didn't speak, and neither did she. There wasn't really anything to say. It took about forty minutes and we were on the spot.

There was an area of ground that was different. The rock was a cracked mass of lava, where I had paced. There were scarred areas on the ground where I had blasted forth with my emotional outburst. Seeing it all, the scars I had left on the land, I felt embarrassed.

She guided me to the center of the lava area. "I am sorry, Nik. Really I am. It breaks my heart to think I caused you such pain. I wish I had done things differently. I need you to hear me."

I smiled awkwardly. "This writing, is going to do this, you know." She nodded. "It's going to drag us through our past. The things you are sorry for, the things I am sorry for, the things we wish we could have done better. It's—" I couldn't continue.

"Tell me again. Why are you doing this?" she asked. "Why are you taking us back through all of this?" Her hand swept the ground below us, pointing out the scars that my emotions had left.

"Because of this," I said, looking at the ground. "So we can heal. So we can move on."

Her eyebrows pinched together as she nodded. "Can you forgive me for this?" she asked quietly.

I drew her close and said, "Yes. I forgive you."

Our hands clasped, we started walking back towards Casita de Soledad.

After a time, she asked, "What do you mean by 'move on'?"

I laughed, "Wouldn't you like to know?" I let go of her hand and started running. "Last one home does the dishes."

I heard a sizzle and a crack and saw a ball of electricity run down the power line towards our home. I stopped and looked back at the charred remains of her clothing smoldering on the ground.

I chuckled, it looked like I would be doing the dishes.

Want more of the adventures of Neutrinoman and Lightningirl? The following is a sample of Episode #3.

Protocol X

Neutrinoman & Lightningirl
A Love Story

Episode #3

Chapter 1

One Foot In Front of the Other
Late Winter 2005, Superstition Mountains, Arizona

MY FEET THUDDED ON THE DIRT TRAIL BELOW ME, DRY and dusty. I was trail running in the Superstition Mountains east of Phoenix, but the Sonoran desert surroundings were pretty much lost to me. I was focusing on one foot at a time, one breath at a time, and had attention for little else.

Endurance training. Actually my life since the "Incident at Yellowstone" (as it was commonly called) had become one big training session. A crashed alien space ship, corpses of aliens, and working alien energy weapons had changed things.

And Licia, she had changed things too.

One foot in front of the other, one breath at a time.

Even as tired as my body was, even as focused as I had to be, I couldn't keep the thoughts of Licia out of my mind. I hadn't seen her in six weeks. Colonel Williams had decided to train us separately for a while. I had to wonder if that wasn't by her request, because it certainly wasn't what I wanted. I figured I was being paranoid, but given what I had experienced in the last few months I was becoming a staunch believer in paranoia, in fact, I think as a q-morph it is a job requirement.

And if I never saw her, how was I going to get her back? This training was taking up nearly all my time; they had even dispensed with the pretense of me working as a janitor at Palo Verde Nuclear Generating Station. I was busy with them all day, every day. I had tried calling her and texting her that first week after she had broken it off. But she didn't answer, and she didn't return my messages.

One foot in front of the other, one breath at a time.

The military had decided that I needed to do endurance training. I ran cross country for a few years in High School, so running it was. The trail running had been my idea. I wasn't going to run circles on some damn military base, I wanted to get out into the desert. Let nature do its work, let it take some of this tension away.

Well, tension isn't the right word. Trauma is. And they had me seeing a therapist for that. I really preferred running and sweating in the beauty of the Arizona desert to sitting in a room with my torturer—err, therapist—talking about how I felt about killing the aliens. Did they think that I wasn't supposed to be traumatized? Did they think I could go through all that and come away with a laugh and a smile?

It's just not that simple.

These thoughts: Licia, trauma, and the aliens kept floating up in my mind. And the running and breathing chased them out. My runs were getting longer and longer and I was finding them to be the only time my mind shut up. You might think sleeping would be good, but I kept dreaming about that blond haired alien with the hole in his chest.

One foot in front of the other, one breath at a time.

HE HAD SHOCKINGLY RED AND WHITE SKIN STREWN WITH freckles. Nestled in his oval face were playful green eyes and he was wearing a big smile when I saw him.

I was on mile twelve of my run, my body worn and past the point where it longed to stop and rest. I rounded a corner and there he was sitting on a rock. The trailhead, and my car, were about a mile further. It was late afternoon on a Wednesday and I hadn't seen anyone on the trail at all.

He was dressed to run, but he didn't look like much of a runner. Too short, too happy. As I rounded a corner, he waved at me. I gave him a brief nod and kept running. I knew who he was, but I wasn't going to say anything.

I heard his feet behind me, the rhythm of his feet faster than mine because of his shorter stature.

"Hey, fella" he began "How's it goin'?" His voice was high with the distinct lilt of an Irish accent.

I was too far into the run to want to talk. I was at that point where the world closed in around me and all I could see was the trail in front of me. I didn't want to talk. I didn't want to interact. I just wanted to keep running.

"Fine," I answered.

"Nice form there, friend. Ya been runnin' long?" He spoke in short, rushed sentences, the words exploding from his mouth.

I ignored him. I thought about increasing my pace, but I didn't really have enough energy left for that. I took a drink from the tube that lead to the water bladder in the little pack on my back. Dehydration was something I had to avoid. I needed to be ready to change to Neutrinoman at any moment, and starting out dehydrated wasn't smart.

"You know," he continued, "I heard ya were a rather decent fella. Kind to strangers. Ready to rescue cats out of trees for little old ladies at the drop of a hat. A real boy scout. But I guess not. Too busy running to talk to one of your own."

I was mad. This was my time. This was what I needed to do for me. Now, I understand why he approached me here, it was one of the only times I wasn't surrounded by military. And I had been expecting this. Williams had briefed me to expect a recruitment pitch. But still I was angry and I really didn't have a problem letting it show.

"What do you want?" I asked as I kept my pace up.

"Ya know. Just a few minutes of your time, Mr. Nichols."

"What for, Mr. Lucky?" I said. I knew he didn't like being called that.

"Hey!" he yelled. I got why he didn't like that name—after seeing him with his red hair perched on the boulder it was obvious. Dress him in a little green suit and shiny black shoes and you'd have yourself a leprechaun. Not that I thought the name Chaosboy was any more dignified.

I looked down and saw that one of my shoes was untied. I grumbled and came to a slow stop, putting my foot on a rock and slowly tying it.

"Lucky break, that." Chaosboy said as he stopped next to me, his breath coming in ragged gasps. He really wasn't a runner.

"You did this?" I asked as I finished tying it.

He shrugged. "I just need a few minutes."

I started walking and took a big drink. I had to cool my body off. After a run that long it wouldn't do to just stop. "So start talking," I said with a sigh. My legs were jelly and it did feel good to be just walking. I was wearing shorts and the little backpack, no shirt, letting my body soak up as much sun as possible. I was in the reactor every day or so at this point, but I always loved the little boost the Arizona sun gave me. My skin was pale, despite all the sun. Radiation and me, we have a unique relationship.

"Toxic, he wants to talk to ya," Chaosboy began. "He's impressed by ya. He thinks you would be just the addition we need at LoVE."

"Love?" I asked.

"Yeah. League of Villains, Extraordinaire. L-O-V-E."

I groaned in response.

"It was you're idea, ya know. Toxic said ya gave him the idea when you asked him if we were 'a league of villains, or something.'"

I groaned again.

"Come on. It's a great name. Ya know, who can argue against love?"

"I'm sorry, what was the point? I got lost in all that blabbering." I felt bad when I said it. Actually, I felt more embarrassed than anything. It was the kind of thing Toxicwasteman would say.

I heard him stop, so I stopped, turned, and faced him. His arms were crossed and he was looking me up and down.

"What?" I asked.

"Toxic, he was right. He said the Battle at Yellowstone and losing your girl would change ya. He said there was a good chance ya would come in. I didn't believe him. But I kinda do now."

I shrugged, turned my back on him, and kept walking. The grumpy tact was proving effective so I decided to keep it up. Besides, I had a lot to be grumpy about.

"So ya gonna come in? Ya gonna hear what he has to say?"

"Why should I?" I kept walking and he trotted up and was now walking besides me.

"Survival, lad. The military has its head so far up their own arses they can't even breathe. Gotta be nimble with this. Military is anything but. We want the same thing. We want those alien bastards dead and gone. Our goals are your goals."

Chapter 2

Recruitment

Late Winter 2005, Superstition Mountains, Arizona

WE WALKED DOWN THE TRAIL IN SILENCE FOR A BIT, PAST tall saguaro cactus, mesquite trees, and stunted sagebrush. It was the kind of location you might film some miners and their donkeys heading out for gold in the 1800s. The sun was warm and I was enjoying the quiet

"It's Chaos, ya know" the red-headed youth said, breaking the silence.

"What?" I asked, stopping and looking at him.

"I am not a boy. I turned twenty-one this year. It's 'Chaos'."

I rolled my eyes and shrugged. I wasn't at all interested in what he wanted to be called. "What is it that you wanted? Aren't we a little off track here?"

"This war with the Arcturian Alliance. It's no conventional war. The stakes are mighty high. The military can't innovate quickly enough. Hell, they need a written order just to take a shite. What this world needs is a small agile group of powerful, dedicated individuals."

"That may be true, but you guys are a league of villains.

I am not a villain. I am not an ends justifies the means kind of guy."

"So, theoretically speaking, what would ya do if ya were confronted with a choice? The stakes are the entire world. You can save it, but one innocent person will die."

"This is ridiculous," I said. "It's never like that. It is never that clear cut."

"Say it was."

I shrugged. "Well, yeah. I would do it."

"Okay, now say it is a thousand people. No, make it a million. Would ya do it knowing a million people would die?"

"No, of course not. I would find another way."

"There is no other way. Ya can save the world, but a million people die."

"This is ridiculous," I said and started walking away.

Chaosboy ran ahead of me and got in my way. "It's not. One million out of six billion; that's like one tenth of one percent. That kind of loss is not acceptable to ya?"

"No."

"We are talking about saving everyone on the planet."

"I'd find another way."

"Ya really are a boy scout. No, I take that back. You're a do-gooder nun. No, that's not good enough. You're Mother freaking Teresa."

"Then I see no reason to come talk to Toxicwasteman."

"It's Toxic, now. We're all going by shorter names. Like, you'd be Neutrino. Nice ring to it, eh?"

I picked him up and put him down on the side of the trail and continued walking.

"I'll make it worth your while," he said from behind me. I could hear him scrambling to catch up. I just kept walking. "I have some information that ya need. I guarantee ya it will be worth it."

He was really starting to annoy me. "What is it?"

"I need your word first."

"Oh…" I began as I stopped and faced him. "Now you want this boy scout's word. Now you care about integrity? When it means you'll get what you want it counts."

He nodded and smiled.

"You have my word that if the information you have is valuable to me I will come and talk to Toxicwasteman."

"And… and ya won't reveal the location of our secret base." He seemed to be warming up to this.

I just stood there with my arms crossed.

He waved his hands in a placating gesture. "Okay. Okay. Ya gave your word, that's good. That's good. I only need one more thing."

HE WANTED PROOF. THE LITTLE GUY WANTED PROOF THAT I was Neutrinoman. It seemed ridiculous to me; he had spent the last twenty minutes pestering me.

I had changed my finger for him until it glowed yellow, but that hadn't been enough. He wanted a full body change. I grumbled but in the end I agreed to do it.

I took us off the trail a bit until I found a large boulder that would afford me some privacy. I had a suspicion that he had other motives for this.

"Satisfied?" I asked him as I stepped around the boulder fully in my neutrino form.

He nodded. "That is impressive."

"So tell me the truth now, why did you have me do this. You knew who I was."

He looked a little sheepish. "Byte's simulation showed there was an 80 to 90% chance ya had a subcutaneous tracking device."

I shook my head. "Why didn't you just ask me?"

He shrugged.

I went back behind the rock still shaking my head. Not out of annoyance at his antics, but because he had been right. I did have a tracking device—at least until I had changed—the military had been expecting this offer.

SEEING CHAOSBOY BEHIND THE WHEEL OF THE HUMMER H2 was kind of funny. He really was short, maybe five foot, and the vehicle just overwhelmed him. We had just left the parking area, headed towards Phoenix.

"So," I began. "What's this valuable information?"

He turned and smiled at me. "You're gonna love this." He then told me my full name, the full name of both my parents, the names of Licia and her parents and the address where we all lived.

"Stop the car," I said, my teeth clenched.

"No. No. Don't freak out, now. We've known for over a month. Took Byte all of ten minutes to get the info."

"Stop the damn car."

"We haven't used that information," he said, glancing at me. "We won't. We were just looking into your background."

"What are the odds that you could survive if I exploded right now?" I asked. "Can you bend probability that much? Stop the car."

He pulled the car over and followed me out. We were still on a little two-lane road in the middle of nowhere. I felt a little dizzy. I walked out into the desert with just enough awareness to step around a big bunch of prickly pear cactus.

"Sorry, fella" he said as he ran out to catch up with me. "I said that wrong."

"You think? You better tell me something, right now or I'll—"

"The media, they've been digging too. Diane Madison, that reporter from WNN, she's got a team on it. They're gonna to find out who ya are, who your family is any day now. Ya need to call them."

I sat down on the sandy ground and got my sat phone out—the military had finally issued me my own satellite phone (aka batphone).

"Told ya it would be worth it," Choasboy said with a grin.

I SAT ALONE IN THE DESERT. I HAD YELLED AT CHAOSBOY until he went back to the Hummer. He seemed hurt, like a puppy who had just done a trick and was anticipating a reward, but got scolded instead. The phone I dialed just kept ringing and ringing. It wouldn't go to voice mail, it was another batphone.

"Hello," she said, finally. My heart thudded in my chest on just hearing that one word.

"Hi, it's Nik."

"Oh. Hi," Licia said.

It was as awkward as I had feared, but there was nothing to be done about it.

"Listen, I need to tell you something. Something important. I..." I trailed off. I missed her and I wanted to do anything but tell her what I needed to tell her.

"What is it, Nik?"

"Where are you? You're not driving or anything?"

"No. I'm on a break from training. You know, they are crazy about this now."

"Yeah, I know. Look, Licia, I am sorry to be the bearer of bad tidings, but I have it on good authority that some reporter is about to find out who we really are."

"Oh..."

"Who we are, where we live, what our parent's names are."

"I... Oh God, this is not good." Her voice was shaking a bit, which made my stomach feel like it was going to fall out.

"No, not good. Everything is going to change. Again." I wanted to hold her and talk to her. She's probably the only other person in the world that could understand what I was feeling right then. It was one thing to be doing the superhero q-morph thing with the shield of anonymity. It was going to be a completely different thing to be doing it under the glare of public scrutiny. Sitting there I was scared and I really had no idea how bad it was going to get.

"I... I better go. I better tell my parents, get my stuff out of my apartment."

"Yeah," I said. "Me too."

There was dead air between us. I wanted to say more, I wanted to plead for a chance to see her, but now was not the time.

"Thanks for telling me, Nik."

"Yeah, of course."

The phone went dead.

I SPENT THE NEXT TEN MINUTES ON THE PHONE. I TALKED to my dad and to Colonel Williams. I didn't talk about

Chaosboy or me having agreed to meet with Toxicwasteman. I am sure Williams could guess.

Maybe it was the specter of being outed as a superhero, maybe something else. But sitting there I was quite paranoid that Chaosboy, or maybe someone else from LoVE, was listening. I didn't want to blow this whole double agent thing before it really got started.

Williams agreed to help. He would coordinate getting my parents someplace where the media couldn't find them. It was going to be a circus.

"Thanks," I said to Chaosboy as I got back to the car.

"Worth it, right?"

I nodded.

"I need ya to melt that down now," he said pointing at the phone.

I shrugged, held the phone out the open window and let my hand, which was holding it, go moderately neutrino and it became a smoldering pile of plastic and electronics. They didn't want the military to track me. So be it.

He then handed me a black bag and told me I need to put it over my head.

"Seriously?" I said.

He nodded. "Secret base, ya know. Ya ain't one of us. Precautions, they got to be taken."

I shrugged, putting it on and putting the seat back on the Hummer. I pretended to sleep, but my mind was way too preoccupied for anything approaching rest.

Chapter 3

Chaosboy

Late Winter 2005, Phoenix, Arizona

I HAD TO WONDER ABOUT THE WHOLE BLACK BAG OVER the head thing. Didn't they know who I was? Didn't they know how I became Neutrinoman? My hearing and sense of smell were better than human norm. Even though I couldn't see, I could tell a lot of what was going on.

Not that it was that surprising. We got on the Superstition Highway and headed west; the sounds of the surrounding buildings and traffic confirmed that. We headed north, on the 101. The afternoon sun made the direction obvious. We ended up at a small airport in Scottsdale.

Hell, I really didn't need to have good senses to tell where we were. Just the noise and the sun was enough, and knowing the area.

But, I played along. This was the game, why the hell not?

I was still in foul mood, and scared. Scared of the life that was coming. Scared that I would never get Licia back, scared of the alien threat of annihilation that hung over it all.

Chaosboy kept up his percussive yammering the whole

way. I couldn't tell if it was to distract me or because he couldn't help himself. Most of it was inane stuff about gambling and sports. But some of it was interesting.

"Toxic is a genius, ya know. That saying, 'the smartest guy in the room.' That's him, alright. It's always him. He's the smartest fella in the room.

"You're gonna love Byte. She's smart and she's... well wait until you see her. She's quite the bird. That'll take your mind off that little ole firefly of yours.

"It's the Greys we need to get. They are from Zeta Reticuli. Mean little bastards. All those stories about alien abductions. That's them. They're the ones. Those stories of anal probes—that ain't bullshit. They get their kicks out of that kind of stuff.

"Ya ever seen a crop circle? Up close? It's freaky. Toxic had me researching them early this year. He's convinced its aliens. Not the Zeta, too creative for them. But some other race. He's thinks they're trying to communicate with us. Maybe trying to help us.

"I heard you been to Area 51. Did you get to see the remains of the ship? Damn military has known about all this for sixty years. They just sat on their hands. What a waste. They could'a been ready for them. But it's down to us, Neutrino. It's down to us."

Once we were on the plane, Chaosboy took the black hood off.

"Thanks," I said.

He nodded. We were in a small gulfstream jet. The shades were all drawn on the windows.

He gave me jeans and a t-shirt in my size, so I changed out of my running clothes and we soon took off and headed north. The sun was up, so even with the shades down the direction we were headed was obvious. We were in the air maybe thirty minutes and we landed.

My heart leapt. Flagstaff. Licia might be up here. It was a stupid and childish thought, and I kinda hated myself for having it. But what is that saying? The heart wants what the heart wants. Duh.

The plane braked really hard and fast and the bag went back on over my head. As soon as we got out of the airplane I knew it wasn't Flagstaff. It was cool, but not freezing cold. We must have gone further north. I suspected the little airport at the Grand Canyon.

The noise as we drove confirmed my suspicions. We weren't in a city the size of Flag. The drive took a while and was slow. We eventually ended up on a dirt road and things got real slow.

"So, why do you believe in him?" I asked when Chaosboy had finally run out of things to babble on about.

"Toxic?" he asked.

"Yeah. Why?"

"Like I said, he's smart. He knows what he's doin'. He's got a plan. And..." He trailed off and I heard him sniff. "All my life people, they never gave me a chance. Being short I got pushed around a lot in school. Got picked last for sports. Girls weren't very interested. But Toxic, he gave me a chance. He gives me responsibility. He trusts me."

"How did you meet?"

"Do you know my origin story?" he asked.

"I don't," I said, although Toxicwasteman had shared some of it on our way to Yellowstone.

"Well, ya know. It was that day. That day we all changed. I was in Vegas down on Freemont Street. They got this crazy zip line that's, like, seventy feet above the street. The street's all blocked off now and is full of folks gone in the head at night. People in costumes. Bands. Things projected on that long-ass awning they have over the street. A lot of fun, really.

"I was really diggin' the zip line and kept doin' it over and over. I was working in Vegas, fixing slot machines. Anyway, Queen was on the awning, singin' 'We Will Rock Ya' while I am sailing above the street. And then the freakiest stuff starts to happen. It's like one of those crazy machines, where the domino falls and triggers the match, which lights the stove, which heats the pot, the steam of which inflates a balloon, which—

"You mean a Rube Goldberg device?" I interjected.

"Yeah, yeah, that. For me it was a Michael Jackson impersonator doin' the moon walk who bumps into the tourist takin' a picture of me, who stumbles in the crowd as he presses the button. His flash blinds this cowboy from Montana who stumbles into a biker from Omaha. The biker takes a swing at the cowboy. Now, some of this I see as I am streaking along. Some of this I put together later. Got lucky and found people who had seen it all.

"Anyway. The cowboy had friends and so did the bikers. A nice, lovely brawl ensues. Security on their goofy Segways head down from just past where the zip line starts. There's this big scaffoldin' and pylons that anchor the thing. The rent-a-cop bumps into a little ole lady who gets her favorite scarf stuck on the little linchpin that anchors the cables to the pylons. She yanks hard and it comes out. Shouldn't matter, right? But there's this bird with a cane in dirty weddin' dress. She loses her balance and stabs out with her cane and the pin pops out.

"Shouldna happened. The odds, they were a billion to

one. But when the thing was built they had trouble with that pin. The worker put some WD-40 on it to get it in place. That bride popped it right out and down came the zip line I was ridin' on.

"So there I am fallin;. My too short a life flashin' in front of me eyes because of some freak accident that should never have happened. Sixty feet up and hard pavement below. I am gonna to die. But I don't. I crash into this booth where people sit around with tubes in their noses sucking on colored oxygen. By some miracle the booth breaks me fall. I walk away unhurt.

"The cosmic rays did their thing. The odds against it happenin' where as high as the odds of me landin' unscathed. I was the luckiest guy in the world. I walked right into the Golden Nugget and started gamblin'. I couldn't lose."

He went silent as we bumped down the road. "You didn't tell me how you met Toxicwasteman," I finally said.

"Oh, that. He heard about the accident and came lookin' for me. I had been hitting Vegas pretty hard, racking up a lot of wins. Too many. The Casinos were banning me. Then they tried to run me out of town. It was like high school all over again. I was surrounded in an alley behind the Golden Nugget. Six big guys. The odds were too far out of my favor to get me out of there without some damage. But I did get lucky. Toxic showed up, showed off, and they went a runnin'." He chuckled before continuing. "I remember what he said. He said, 'You and me, we're gonna go far, kid.'"

Chapter 4

The Pitch

Late Winter 2005, LoVE Base, Near the Grand Canyon

THE LAST PART OF THE RIDE WITH CHAOSBOY WAS VERY slow and very rough. We eventually went into a tunnel before parking.

"Okay," he said. "Ya can take that thing off."

I do and there is not much to see. The headlights on the Land Rover are illuminating the form of Tom Tyree. Tall, gaunt, and middle-aged he is standing about ten yards in front of the vehicle with his arms crossed. We are in a cave about twenty feet in diameter, with a tunnel behind us and a tunnel in front of us where Tom is standing.

I ignored Chaosboy and got out and walk to Tom. "So, I'm here. What is it that you wanted to say?"

He looked me up and down, frowned, and then smiled. "Is it any wonder she's had enough of you? Always jumping right in, never any foreplay."

I smiled and crossed my arms matching his pose and expression and just stood there. I was annoyed, but letting him see it wasn't going to help. Actually I was very annoyed. How is it that everyone always seemed to know my business?

"All right then," he said. "I'll give you the tour."

He took me down the tunnel, harshly illuminated by bare bulbs strung along the wall. We came out into a large cave that was about fifty feet in diameter with a relatively flat dirt floor. There were several tunnels exiting this cave in various directions. In the center of the cave was a round table with chairs set around it. Sitting at it was Charles Calvin, aka Dr. Cheese. He had his round rimmed glasses and lab coat on.

"You know Dr. Cheese," Tom said.

I nodded and gritted my teeth. I disliked the guy immensely. His super power was the production of enzymes. Doesn't sound like much, does it? But think about it. Enzymes are biological substances that cause chemical reactions. So, the magic that turns milk into cheese: enzymes. Almost all chemical reactions in your body involve enzymes.

Dr. Cheese reached up and took my hand shaking it. His hand was moist and limp; I wanted to wipe it off, but didn't. He smiled but didn't speak.

We've had our run-ins. He once infected several orchards of oranges in Florida. He would walk past the trees touching each one and infecting it with an enzyme. That enzyme infected the tree and transformed the oranges, turning them poisonous. The poison was subtle though and wasn't detected until the juice was in the market. The compound in the juice lowered inhibitions, kind of like being very drunk, and resulted in chaos all over the country for a few weeks.

He never did ask for anything. Once I finally caught up

with him, he claimed he had been experimenting. Actually he called it, "my little social experiment."

See why I wanted to wipe my hand? God knows what kind of enzyme he just infected me with, and what kind of chemical reaction it could cause in my body.

I hated the guy, I really did. But I kept my mouth shut and followed Tom.

"This is Byte," Tom said as he introduced me to an attractive woman of about thirty. She was dressed simply, in jeans and a black turtleneck, but she moved in a sensuous way that was quite alluring. "That's B.Y.T.E., you know like computers. Digital something or another." His hand waved vaguely at the racks of computer gear behind her.

Byte smiled, and pushed her shoulder length blond hair behind her right ear. "A pleasure," she said shaking my hand. Her grip was firm and confident.

"Byte here is the nerve center of our operations," he said. "She handles communications, research, and simulations."

"Simulations?" I asked.

"We do a lot of mathematical modeling," she said, "looking at odds and probabilities. Attempting to predict future patterns based on historical information. Data mining for unseen trends, that kind of thing." She spoke with an English accent that to my untrained ear, sounded like she was well educated.

"We model everything," Tom said. "We don't take a move unless we like what we see in the simulations. In fact—"

"You're going to want to see this," Byte said looking at me and interrupting Tom. She pointed at a large monitor hanging from the ceiling and it turned on. On the screen was Diane Madison, her perfectly coifed hair, and plastic smile making me feel uncomfortable in way I couldn't quite explain.

"Join us at 7 pm central, 8 pm pacific for a WNN exclusive report: Neutrinoman Unmasked. We delve into the real life of this real superhero and explode the secrecy surrounding him and other quantum-morphs."

The screen muted as a commercial for Viagra came on. I stood there staring and blinking at the screen while some grey haired guy talked earnestly about how happy he was now that his penis works better.

I felt a gentle squeeze of my arm and looked at Byte. The look on her face appeared to be compassionate, genuine. It made me wonder what she was doing here. I looked around and saw that Tom had left and was talking to Dr. Cheese. I looked at her face and head closely. I couldn't see any equipment on her. Like a headset so she could hear what was on WNN. Or a remote so she could turn the TV on.

"You're a..." I stammered.

"Q-morph," she said, nodding her head. "I was a geek in a server room when the cosmic rays hit. I was installing some new servers and some bad wiring sent the internet flowing through me. Not enough electricity to kill me or anything, but it turned my legs to jelly and I woke up a few hours later and could sense the data going through the air."

I nodded in awe. "Were you bit or anything?"

"You're wondering about the third element. Cosmic rays, plus freak accident, plus gene changing catalyst. Like the rat in your case."

I nodded.

"I had gotten a flu vaccination right before the accident. Near as I can figure, that was the third element."

I nodded, still dazed by where I was, who I was with, and what I had just seen on the TV.

"Do you need to sit?" she asked taking my arm and guiding me to the table.

When Chaosboy had told me that my secret was about to come out, I had believed him. It was kind of inevitable. Everyone knew I worked at Palo Verde. Everyone knew that Neutrinoman used it as home base. Starting with a list of employees and with a little effort it was going to be found out.

But, now that it was happening I felt extremely disoriented. I didn't sign up to be a superhero and to this point, anonymity had been one of the only things keeping me sane, giving me a shred of a normal life. And now? I had no idea how I would cope with the world knowing who I was.

"How about some cheese?" Dr. Cheese asked, sliding a plate towards me. The smell was intoxicating and a welcome distraction. "I made it myself," he added. I pushed the plate away.

THE PLAN HAD BEEN A SIMPLE ONE. THE MILITARY WAS expecting Toxicwasteman or one of his people to contact me. When they did, I would agree to a meeting, learn all I could, and then alert the military to their location. They would swoop in and take them all into custody.

Sitting there smelling Dr. Cheese's cheese, reeling from the upcoming outing of me as Neutrinoman, I just had to laugh. It was such a simplistic plan. So easy. So logical.

Except Chaosboy had given me a chance to warn my family. I knew I was supposed to be the hero and they were supposed to be the villains, but it was Toxicwasteman that saved the day when we last met in Yellowstone. He had used me as a pawn in his plan, but he had gotten the job done.

But, what if he was using me as a pawn again? What if he had arranged for this little Diane Madison thing, this unmasking of a superhero?

I was so confused. But sitting there with Dr. Cheese watching him nibble on pieces of cheese was not doing me any good.

"What's with the lab coat," I asked him.

"Huh?" he asked, pushing his round glasses back into position and brushing at his short grey hair. He was a chubby little dude, built like a fireplug.

"You are always wearing a lab coat. What is up with that?"

"Well, I am a doctor, after all," he said with a sniff.

"Yeah. Doctor." Chaosboy said as he sat down and started eating the cheese. "Oh, man. Cheesy, you've out-done yourself."

"You were a podiatrist before the accident," I said. "Why wear a lab coat now? We're in a cave. There's no one else here."

He pulled the white coat tight, monogrammed on the pocket was, "Dr. Cheese." He blinked rapidly, his eyes twitching around before meeting mine. "Do you really want to know?"

I nodded. I didn't know if I did, but staying trapped in my head was not a good thing.

"Branding," he said with a nod, before picking up what looked like a piece of Havarti. My mouth was watering; I was more than a little hungry.

"Branding?" I asked.

"Yes, branding. Depending on how all this turns out,

there might be some value in my name and image. Endorsements, appearances, product sales. The lab coat is my brand. So I wear it, you never know when you might be seen." His hand hovered over the plate of cheese; he seemed to be deciding between a piece of cheddar or another Swiss. "Are you sure you don't want some?" he asked.

I was worried about them poisoning me, but I was hungry, and the cheese did smell fantastic.

"You know," Tom began as he sat down beside me. "You really ought to consider branding yourself. You could be making a mint off of endorsements right now. Neutrinoman energy drinks, Neutrinoman comic books and movies. LoVE has a team of lawyers on retainer; if you were to join us, we could make all of that happen."

My hand darted out, almost against my volition, and snagged a piece of Swiss. It was amazing; fresh and sharp, rich and creamy. I rationalized that if they had wanted to poison me they already had. If Dr. Cheese had wanted to infect me he could have done it when we shook hands. "Wow," I said, surprised when I heard myself speak.

"No one does cheese like Dr. Cheese," Byte said as she sat down on the other side of me. She placed a large tablet computer in the middle of the table on a stand. She smelled of roses with a hint of patchouli. I didn't recall her having that scent on when we met. I found it a bit distracting.

"Let's do this," Tom said. As I sat there eating some of the best cheese I had ever tasted, Tom and the rest of them made their pitch.

THE LIGHTS IN THE CAVE DIMMED, SEEMINGLY OF THEIR own accord, with a single light shining from above on the table. This left the cave outside the circle of light dark and murky. On the tablet appeared the letters L. o. V. E. in 3D slowly rotating.

"This table," Tom began after clearing his throat, "is round for a reason. Like King Arthur of legend everyone here has a voice. Everyone here contributes. Everyone here knows the plan. We have no secrets from each other."

Tom got up and slowly walked around the table. There were eight chairs, but only five us there.

He stopped behind Dr. Cheese, his hands resting briefly on the man's thick shoulders. "Doc here is our medic and our chef. His enzymatic superpowers are useful in a variety of situations. He can cause destruction if need be, or get us through a door quietly and quickly. His enzymes can harm or help depending on our needs."

With a smile Tom moved to Chaosboy. "Chaosboy here is our luck. Everything, and I mean everything, goes better with him. He is our eyes and ears in the world, our talent scout, and the first one to join me."

He moved on to Byte, his hands caressing her hair before going to her shoulders. "Byte here is the nerve center of our operation. She can get us through any firewall, can disable any security system, retrieve for us any data, and takes care of managing our finances."

"I," he began standing behind his own seat, "am the brains of the operation, and sometimes the brawn. I keep us on mission and on task."

He then moved behind my chair and put his hands on my shoulders. "You, Neutrino, you could be our most powerful weapon. The aliens fear you, fear your power, and with good reason. We need you to save this planet. We, literally, cannot do it without you."

He sat back down. "Our mission is singular and focused: destroy the alien threat; save the planet; have a party." After a dramatic pause he looked me directly in the eyes and asked, "Will you join us, Nik?"

Want more? The next episode of "Neutrinoman and Lightningirl: A Love Story" will be out soon. To keep abreast of the latest news, sign up for my newsletter at neutrinoman.com (use the yellow box on the right side of the screen).

Acknowledgements

THIS ONE HAS BEEN A LONG TIME COMING. I LOVE THESE superhero/love stories. I love the characters. I love the quirky mix of action and romance with a few laughs here and there, a bit serious now and then. But it takes an effort, a big one, to finish one of these and push it out to the world.

It's a good effort. A satisfying effort. Like running a race or climbing a mountain. But just like Nik Nichols, I'm not alone, I need help. It takes a lot of support to write a book.

So, many thanks to my fabulous team of beta writers: John Bifano, Roni Hornstein, Chris Kalinich, Michele Lytle, Susanne One Love, and Aleia N. O'Reilly.

Great work, as always, by Diana Cox, my proofreader (www.novelproofreading.com).

An additional call out to my wife, Aleia. She supports me and listens to my stories, listens to me prattling on endlessly about writing and publishing, and always, always loves me. I can't imagine my life without her!

And thanks to you for reading. Stay tuned, more of the adventures of Neutrinoman and Lightningirl coming soon.

About the Author

ROBERT J. MCCARTER IS VERY COMFORTABLE WRITING about characters as long as one of those characters is not himself. Actually, Robert is anything but comfortable speaking (or writing) of himself in the third person—he finds it pretentious and silly.

So, let's drop all that usual bio crap.

Hi, my name is Robert, and I make things up and write them down. As a reader you may be interested in knowing something about me, so here goes:

I am a computer programmer by trade and have been for a very long time. I wrote my first program over thirty years ago and never stopped. I found the dramatic arts in high school, which got me through that rather daunting rite of passage, and fell in love with the arts. After high school, I started writing really bad poetry about how lonely I was and how clueless I was about the opposite sex (which, fortunately for all of us, I burned). After that my writing turned towards fiction.

I have written sporadically for several decades, and in what is, in all probability, part of a mid-life crisis, I started writing seriously (i.e. regularly) a few years ago. I have always been drawn to the arts (acting, photography, fractal art, and writing) and find that I am most happy when I am being as creative as possible. Thus, all the sitting alone at my computer making things up.

My writing is colored by my technical (i.e. geek) past as well as my age. I'm no youngster, so themes of death, grief, and change tend to creep into my writing (Okay, that's an understatement). Also, having been trained as an engineer, I like things to make sense and do my best to keep the hand waving to a minimum.

If you asked me to succinctly say something to summarize my writing style, I would tell you to go buzz off. But then, after profuse apologies, I would say: "I write humanist-geek, character-oriented sci-fi with heart."

I live in the middle of a Ponderosa Pine forest in the mountains of Arizona with my beautiful wife and my ridiculously adorable dog.

If you'd like to get a hold of me, use the contact form on my website (RobertJMcCarter.com/contact-me/). I'd love to hear from you, really I would.

Oh, and if you want the inside scoop on my writing, sign up for my newsletter (I won't share your name and emails are infrequent—around once a month). You can sign up using the blue box on the right of my website at RobertJMc-Carter.com.

Also by Robert J. McCarter

Novels in the "Ghost's Memoir" world:
Shuffled Off: A Ghost's Memoir, Book 1
Drawing the Dead
To Be a Fool: A Ghost's Memoir, Book 2

Novellas (short novels) in the
Neutrinoman and Lightningirl Series:
Meteor Attack!
    Lightningirl and Neutrinoman, A Love Story. Episode 1
Toxic Asset
    Lightningirl and Neutrinoman, A Love Story. Episode 2
Protocol X
    Lightningirl and Neutrinoman, A Love Story. Episode 3
    (Coming soon)

Novelettes
Probability: Resolve
The Turing Test Will Be Televised
Ghost Hacker, Zombie Maker